QUERENCIA WINTER 2023

Querencia Press, LLC
Chicago Illinois

QUERENCIA PRESS

ISBN

978 1 959118 14 5

.

www.querenciapress.com

First Published in 2023

**Querencia Press, LLC
Chicago IL**

Printed & Bound in the United States of America

OTHER TITLES FROM QUERENCIA

CONTENTS

POETRY

The British Museum – Alice Louise Lannon (she/her)

We scan the floor plan and find 'Africa' located in the basement.
The sign does not mention blood.
It only states that some artefacts were

acquired

as a direct result of British military expeditions.
We want to keep her alive. We've come here on a quest. We
examine glassy cabinets until we find a card that says
Country of origin: Kenya.
We text her brother:
'Do you think she'd like us to steal back this spear?'

Steal, acquire, fact, fiction: it's all the same.

I see us smashing the case to shards and running away, charging out
of the white marble museum with this ancient weapon against hurt.
As if by laying it to rest at her feet, she too will return to us.

But she didn't want to stay.
She wanted to go home.
She returns to Kenya in a box,

as planned.

The newspapers write: *she was, she was, she was*
but I cannot archive her smile,
leave her to become story under glass.

Yet again you are not invited to the meeting – Alice Louise Lannon
(she/her)

They tell you

*don't worry if you see cigar smoke coming out from under the door,
it's the all boys club today I'm afraid*

and they all laugh, as if this is ridiculous. The one with the soft
brown eyes joins the joke, and you realise you can't even trust your
allies. So kind in private, now he won't meet your small wounded
mammal gaze. You wish you had a shell.

Other times they tiptoe
around the fact that you are a woman,

as if you had not noticed your size in a room with 10 large men. Like
you hadn't realised they could hold you down if they

desired.

Determined to win,

you buy an instruction manual. There is no test you have not passed
with flying colours. The book tells you to do things like

lean in and *be direct*

so you stop with the tiptoe and start saying no. You stand up
forthright and all you receive are flinches. You know you are
becoming the difficult one and everyone else knows it too. You hate
having to be so defensive, your new hard edges, your robot voice to
cover the quivers. In the evening, safe on your sofa you hold a wine
glass and scroll for an escape route.

Child minding,
nursery nurse,
flower arranging,
you just want to be soft again.

But you keep going back, your body becoming more and more
mechanical.

Would you mind picking up some bacon rolls for the boys?
You are a copywriter and marketing assistant. You are a vegetarian.
Customers phone and don't believe a word you say, ask to speak to
the manager or just anyone who is a man,

anyone but you

dash out the door of your flat each morning, down the stairs and
dash back up again, lurching over the toilet bowl, heart beating,
palms sweating in the anticipation. You are often late.

You dream about pushing your boss off a cliff

and watching him fall in slow-motion. Him becoming smaller and
smaller, as small as he made you feel.

You smile as you watch.

Sitting at your computer,

again you feel it rising in your stomach, in the silence and sweat and
testosterone, and run to the bathroom. It has a picture of a person
with a skirt on, so you are the only one who uses it. Everyone
intensely pretends they can't hear, whilst silently filing the
information, just as they pretend not to notice you have a uterus.
They probably think you're pregnant.

The cleaning man takes out all the bins,

except the sanitary bin in the women's bathroom.

He simply mops around it. You wonder if this is yet another screaming unspoken thing. Time passes and you agonize in an awkward, impossible impasse. Knotted stomach, churning as you clench your body tight at your desk. Your hands are typing, but in your head you play out how you could acquire the bin bags and smuggle the contents of the bin out of the building and locate the larger bin to put it all in. Time passes and you grow more and more tense. You are frozen so do nothing about this embarrassing,

escalating,
female,
situation.

When eventually it is underlined in a private meeting how *unprofessional* your sporadic bouts of vomiting are,

you try very hard not to cry and then you call it. You all go to the pub for leaving drinks. You are surprised, but then again, these are guys who *want to do the right thing*. You select a pint even though you prefer white wine, tell yourself this will be the last time.

As you raise your glass,

all you can think of is the six months' worth of decaying tampons in the bathroom bin, the lingering legacy you left the men to deal with.

Aisling/Angel – Alice Louise Lannon (she/her)

Conas atá tú?
Cé thusa?

I am foreign:
I cannot name
        the smell of white silk,
the touch of incense
                        and the weight of history.

Aisling,
angel—I'm sure it would have
been so beautiful
            to be you.

Éire is
        a nameless feeling
in my veins,
        but your tongue would
        give it shape

I want to lay flowers
                    but
                I'm not sure I can
lay claim to this land
In a language it can understand.

She looks heavenward
                        through lace,
weaves hearts
through harp strings

and knows her namesake:

Fleetingly,
        a flutter of wings and
I wonder,
what it would have been like
to be
                Aisling.

Siren's Song – Alexandria Perdue (she/her)

Nostalgia be the name of a siren's call. Coercing you down under murky memories and deep sentiments; feelings that have not seen the surface in years and emotions that can no longer serve you on land.

For the ocean of time is a lost world, swelling and crashing, angry and unsettled with regret, with want, with fear.

Be wary of its deceptive song, for its melody is sweet, but its lyrics are bait; hooks and lines meant to pull you under the current.

It is okay to remember, but do not stick around to hear the song's end. Take with you only what you can carry; a single shell with the faint call hidden in its spiral; a mere token to honor the past but not to be overtaken by its waves.

For you will be stuck in a cycle of drowning if you do not look forward towards the shore.

Fall – Alexandria Perdue (she/her)

The roses had already begun to wilt the day
she brought the bouquet home. He had
given them to her half-heartedly, with an
awkward thrust.

They were meant to be an apology but felt
more like the resigning of an already broken
treaty.

The bouquet now sat in a yellow-stained vase
on the windowsill overlooking the backyard.
The autumn colors danced about as she forced
her gaze past the flowers, watching the leaves fall
and flutter in the wind.

The warm tones would soon be nothing but
muddied decay at the base of the trees, just as
the vibrant roses would soon be nothing but
withered and gnarled petals littering the floor
beneath the window.

He hadn't even muttered those two words
when he'd handed them over. Those two words
that had become so predictable in his
vocabulary over the past year. Words the rolled
off his tongue without true thought or sincerity.

The gesture was meant to be enough, a thin life line thrown over the boat to try and save the last remnants of the relationship. But what pulled on the line now was dead weight. She had no longer the strength to fight, to care, to forgive.

She ran a finger aimlessly over the engagement ring she wore, fidgeting with and twisting it until it ultimately slid off and clattered on the table.

Movement in her periphery pulled her gaze back from the falling leaves she'd been honed in on, and her eyes slid to the floor.

The first petal had fallen.

Seoul – Ensol Baek (she/her)

home is the city
where spring is only the half-melt black sludge beneath your feet.

ugly, stilted line-breaks,
stolen jargon, out-of-place
paraphernalia, like pamphlets
that soak up the lipids
that sink.

naked, faceless torsos
belonging nowhere, advertising
numbers which disappear
—my language turned grey jibberish.

smudges shedding multitudinous
turned pulp in puddle, exhausts condensed.

where bodies live dismembered
where bad english, bad poetry lives
poisons you savor, these bad habits of your tongue
home: where the spirit-box-concrete-plastic-radio
forever plays static at your request of ghostly song.

17 – Ensol Baek (she/her)

It was something like the white butterfly I took, forgoing
Sleep, dissolving; self-fed and muted
—when I would starve then engorge myself
in numbing pattern, reassuring,

Picturing every corpuscle aflame
In perpetual summer-shimmer, urban haze
Wearing the basic symptoms like a necklace
—blistered knuckles, bruised back, anaemic vertigo, dazed high.

Fluorescent-lit all night, the white ceiling bubbled and broiled;
Curling kaleidoscopic; boomerang insults impaled-confirmed.
Insomniac nausea, acidic empty or sweet unswallowed,
Porcelain cruel and cold; *there would be no peaceful drowning—*

Lost in the white nights, distracted-sleepless-paralysed,
No break. *Crush, snap the plastic joint, pop the stitches at her neck.*
Broke the lying breathless and made out, survived.

Like a tattoo of a comma gotten some long time ago,
there lies a wound enclosed. A breath remembered.

Jeju – Ensol Baek (she/her)

It had been a second since the sun had set
And night's freedom was denied: spring camellia came raining—
April petals dropped and blazed the grounds anew;
Crushed under army boots deep into soil
Onto ash onto lava onto sand onto stone
Bleeding, squeezed dry, into island's every pore
Seeped into seas,
Dying winds red—
Then the dead were easy to blame.

Beneath the unknowing footsteps of tourists that pass by
Between *surfers* and *hikers* and *rented-cars-drivers*
On *beaches* on *cliffs* in *forests* in *natural wonders*—
Drenched red are the gaps of words unallowed.

The Death of Winter – Liz Yew (she/they)

Leaves fall as lakes freeze
Lulled by the death of the last Autumn scene
Life halts with that soulless winter breeze

Unsuspected

Farewell to fleeting nature
As we promise to reunite
In forms we no longer capture

What was to be expected
When winter wind whispers
That ghostly harmony of sirens allured

With Spring and Summer trapped in Kore's garden
All was hollow and frozen

Indeed, we meet again
Blossomed anew
As we begin to comprehend

The Day Loving Kindness Killed Us… – T. Lydia McKinney
(they/them/she)

I sold my soul to
serenity

my sister, Trinity

was so happy to see me

her tears bled onto my
chest

At best, she only knew
the version of a portrait

my family painted a
man

never abandons his
family

and

when famine fills the
belly

with boatfuls of
fictitious fabrications

as fake as an orgasm or

anything which has him
believe

this

is what life is

he will look upon me
and ask

how can I live as
righteously

as you?

I'll say

"seek first the kingdom
of God"

A nod in agreement
nullifies our exchange

it's strange how a
manger could hold such
blissful anger

The drummer beats a
banger

the danger is coming,
repent now

or resent yourself so we
can see

how apathetic and
uninterested you are in
fully investing

At best, nothing I say is
credible

This bread, if edible (and
gluten free)

will feed the multitude

Ultimately, we starved
ourselves

saw so much to eat

we spent our time trying
to pick and choose

hoarding resources, basic
human needs

like water, connection

protection from the
convection of anger
culminating

from the baby born in
perfection, but

gender and race set a
pace

a place at a table we
became too bougie to set

I bet God if

She would tell me why she
was sorry

I

would save us all... the
fall of man was shortly
after

I gathered

the bones of universal
forefathers

forgot them in the crust

must

life always be full of
mourning?

She says "no"
I listen to glistening
snowfall, although cold

She embraces me

in everlasting solstice

This

is how the cookie
crumbles

I lay

in the grave awaiting
the third day

when spring comes

I will rise again.

The Most Wonderful Time (2020) – T. Lydia McKinney
(they/them/she)

This Christmas, I

will celebrate like a holiday pagan

Instead of

"thank you, Jesus"

this Christmas shows gratitude   to all   of

                                                      my nothing

                                                      my thoughts

drift me recklessly

        round the last curve   of the year,

             in a car   I couldn't pay for

                                will open my eyes

                                wishing I was anywhere

                                          but here

                                          but

this Christmas, I am   present

remember
it is
the most wonderful time of
the year   the part where it ends

                                        and

as the sea broadens,
on this
        the third day of Christmas

three French hens (Oui, Myself, and I)

spend silent night in hell

me   tells myself

'better than showing up

                    at their house'   here
                                    healing

chestnuts on hellfire I can extinguish

                         anytime it gets out
                         of Amazon

the rain   hasn't fallen since Autumn

           and ♪"all I want for Christmas is U"nion
                              was it Gabrielle?

or Gabriel

who made this day marry?
                    Mariah   can't carry you

Stop asking black womxn to perform
                         your Christmas miracles
           whyon'tcha   sing
                         your own song
                              Bela   -fonte be

                    the icy sleet and snow

                    I tried to let go but

this Christmas, I
couldn't

wouldn't be here

without the friends and family   I miss

and I do   miss my family
I just don't want to be   a bird   -den, fly away
                                                  an array of
              Christmas decay held   in a day of memories
                                                  won't heal me

When Christ was born,
three 'wise' men   gifted   gold, frankincense,
                                              and myrrh

to a baby

but since they were men
          they were
          therefore wise...why?
                    By the way
          'Christ wasn't born
          on Christmas'

          my mother reassures me, so
                                        nothing about

this Christmas   actually makes sense
                                  Although Pence
                                          is no longer
                              in the Hwyte House

my black, still decks the halls
with boughs   of ancestors who
                         built them
                                 this Christmas,

corporations continue to capitalize

selling gluttony to needy children

                              as greedy humans brag
                              about coming from rags

                              to new Jag in the driveway

                                  feeding price tags
                                  to the homeless

this Christmas, still   a frag grenade

                              of broken treaty and unpaid reparation

                                  paperwork crafted from the pulp

                    of trees   losing their lives
to disease
and disaster

the bells don't jingle

and we can't   even mingle about it

This Christmas,
A holy night awaits   the drummer

                              solstice begins
                                      bereavement
and all I can do...   is breathe.

waiting to reap – **Dillon Charli** (they/them)

I am stitching
Ever so slowly
The pieces of my life
To the tapestry that surrounds me
Sewing hand over hand
Sheet to skin
Breaking threads
And starting over again

Warehouse Worker, 2020 – Dillon Charli (they/them)

My feet are calloused and bruised
After a hard day's night, I am left limping
My spine holding a lifetime of tension;
If I sit, I may not rise again.
People tell me that I am young
That I should not have this pain
As if, at their words it will dissipate
They don't understand the true meaning of age
How much weight these aching bones have carried
How many miles these bleeding feet have journeyed
Young in years but not in stories
Life has not given me the luxury of naivety
Has not spared me the trials which precursor wisdom
Poverty does not care for youth or beauty
It is the great equalizer of generations
The founder of "fortitude" and "tenacity"
The reason for my "resilience"

Say Your Name – Dani De Luca (she/her)

meet me beyond sleep
hold a handful of chokeberries
and dead petals, cut from my once-
blonde hair, in your mouth and
wet them alive

sit next to the butcher of things,
press into his soft places, see how
his vision blurs through the breaths
he cannot take

remember the cop in the cornfield
and the Krav Maga master in the pizzeria
who de-storied his victims 'names but
re-storied their crushed ribs on closed fists

tell me my name means anything but
God is my Judge, tell me it means
I Hoped to be Fire but am Water
instead, tell me water is better to be

know we will always be crossing
and losing, that the blood on our
breasts will dry but seep beneath
our skin and story there, first

make your presence a ministry of
profound love, sew skin roses
next to hurt places so there is
beauty where pain lives, then

say your name
shear your name
sow your name
again and again

Unsweet – Dani De Luca (she/her)

Yesterday, I thieved my son's treat bucket
and plowed its top layer.
People call it stress-eating. I call it:
Snickers-smashed-like-Mahsa's-*re-educated*-face eating.
Twizzlers'-legs-forced-apart eating.
Sour-Patch-Kids-of-January-6 eating.
Starburst-after-AR-15-sends-students-skyward eating.
Payday-equality-for-all-women eating.
Now and Later-we-remember-the-war eating.
Zero-tolerance-for-black-boys-growing-past-death eating.
Smarties-who are-you-to-legislate-my-body eating.
I ingest the putridly saccharine stories
and wait and wait and wait
for sweetness.

Under a Strawberry Moon, Rising – Dani De Luca (she/her)

The sage of thyme within
spills berried ribbons be-
tween our legs that whet
the lips & tongue there.

Thyme does not forget
the pull of the moon on
the waters of women.
How it churns the salt &

silt of pasts & futures til
it brights the now— **a**
supered timepiece in astral
soil. She holds us, whispers:

Remember what's inside

the oh in moan
the lead in bleed
the on in swan

End – Dani De Luca (she/her)

I only befriend the tender
who commend
the slender lavender
and suspend
the calendar's ascendance.
Such hearts tend surrender.
Upend the
pendulum of endurance,
dear friend.
Bend where you feel like ending.
Send me
your life's renderings, so I
may mend
its splendid tendrils and
scend you
forward. You, dear legend,
your wending—
a pendant round my neck.

Endless.

Untitled – Wesley R. Bishop (he/him)

Alabama on my mind
as passing by prison-labor on roadside
beautifying dividers green.

Pants are orange and white,
stripped to show, reflecting light.
Alabama, ever the genius

in stealing labor not theirs.

Untitled – Wesley R. Bishop (he/him)

Nature poets never seem to fail
to capture beauty as they do their communing.

And, so, I try, but always fail
and can only think about how my feet sound stomping

when I sat, on cracked commode at Alabama *Aldi's*
and tried to scare cockroaches away
who suddenly appeared from behind can of tumbling trash.

STOMP. STOMP. STOMP.
SCUTTLE. SCUTTLE. SCUTTLE.

Dancing with nature in communal spaces.

Untitled – Wesley R. Bishop (he/him)

I dreamt last night we were all doomed to die at the stroke of three
(not midnight, far too cliché)
but could be saved, if and only if, someone uttered your name
and saw you as worthy of being saved.

In those panicked hours we came to realize how much celebrity
mattered.
Go-Fund-Me campaigns for the lonely sprouted like weeds
and name-insurance-plans assembled.

And we waited to see who would say whose name.

I had her name on my tongue
and she had my name bouncing out
and we hugged
and waited, praying,
for the nameless.

Untitled – Wesley R. Bishop (he/him)

Jesus revival in Walmart parking lot. "Jesus Saves!" gospel singers inform.
But, too, "Save at Walmart!" signs declare.

Those cart wranglers, orange vested pushing flashing silver mounts, cause me to duck
when I hear *BANG*!

gun… gun… gun…

I fret. But fear not! Just carts, temporarily, out of control.
What do I have to fear? We are all going to be saved!

saved… saved… saved…

singers intone because somewhere, somewhen, a coupon was nailed to a cross.

Slumbering Song – K.L. Green (she/her)

The Darkness of night
Plays concert hall
To the two sleeping forms
Beside me.
The first splits the night
With long slurping gulps
Through the straw that stretches
Into a well of dreams below.
The second is a field mouse
Ensconced in petal bed
So gentle a sight
Yet gurgles out a grizzly growl.
Two sleeping forms
Both far gone yet somehow
Still in sync in their rhythms
Even now.
And me as I lay
Pondering their movements
The lento e andante
Melodic solo and cacophonous chorus
I drift into my own instrument
To sing out sweet song.

Ribbon – Ann Kammerer (she/her)

I hate
the hot gravel voice,
spitting like pebbles
beneath the tires
of a three-speed Schwinn.

I hate
the welled eyes,
the smack,
the cries of
"Mommy, no.
I'll be good,"
as shouts of
"Shut up.
You're bad,"
send shoppers
scattering
in the aisles.

Years ago,
a teacher said
I should add a sun,
green trees,
and pretty flowers
to my Mother's Day art.
"That's me," I said,
"and my mommy."
She placed a slender hand
on my shoulder
as I scratched
two stick figures
on a ribbon
cut from gray paper,
their claw-shaped feet
perched on broken letters,
proclaiming
"Best Mom in the World."

TV minutes – Ann Kammerer (she/her)

Dad watched TV.
Mom got mad.
They argued.
Most days.
He said she should do more.
She said she did plenty.
Sometimes she said
she'd been better off
marrying that Nazi,
the one from the
Battle Creek prison camp,
the place she worked
during World War II.

"At least he loved me," Mom
cried.
"You just love TV."
Veins popped on Dad's neck.
"Don't nag me," he shouted.
"I'm watching the news."
He swore about politicians.
He cursed Republicans.
He railed about Nixon,
and Watergate,
and the 18-minute gap.

"Who cares?" Mom
screamed.
"Care about me."
Dad's face flamed.
His chin squared.
"Just shut up," he yelled.
He threw things.
She cried.
We ran into the backyard
to hide in a clearing,
surrounded by pines,
our bare legs pricked
by fallen needles
as we added
to our collection of cones.

penthos & earl grey – Sarah Jeannine Booth (she/her)

the smell of earl grey tea transports me back in time
i'm 21 again in my best friend's flat
in nelson, new zealand, december 2010—*summer*
the whackiest christmas i've ever had—*hot, BBQ fare,*
walking through town (shoes optional!) with blisters on my toe
pads

before lockdowns, health passports, and government panic
we roamed free on the south island with zero care
every morning, i'd enjoy this familiar cup
that sweet bergamot aroma, tantalizing my nostrils, enticing my
tastebuds
a heady taste of home on the other side of the world

to this day, i don't know what went wrong between us
everyone always cited irreconcilable   distances,
but that doesn't check out when we'd write each other letters
or long facebook messages in our unique hybrid concoction of
english, with nods to *angus, thongs, and full-frontal snogging*

so no, i don't think it was a matter of belonging to opposite
hemispheres,
just a bifurcated path in opposite directions
and differing opinions on the meaning of bests
so yes, a sip of earl grey tea transports me back to christmas 2010
tinged with penthos now that we're no longer friends

look up – Sarah Jeannine Booth (she/her)

some days, it's true, there is nothing left to give
you plumb the depths & come up with pocket lint

you cannot pour from an empty cup, so fill, fill,
fill your soul with all the delights you know

all the grace & gusto you possess
rise above the murk & mess—sing your lark's song

spring for joy, harness happiness
even when you're empty, even when you're lacking

there is good if you just peer outside into the world
then look within. no quick results or haphazard fixes

it's alright to weep
(the gift of tears) but then look up

be it by the light of the moon
or the first raise of morning, gold to blue.

Tomorrow – Aya Sunga Askert (she/her)

Tomorrow
when your hands are frail
your murmurs fail
In grand éclat
your words I'll cite
your song I'll sing
for our love's might

By hundreds of flickering embers
to everyone I'll tell
The zealous sentiments you uttered
once, twice, a hundred quivers
Every time I griped about
the despicable furrows on my face
the fading lustre in my eyes
the implacable grey hair
flourishing on my head

You said:
Tomorrow
when your hands are frail
your murmurs fail
Do not fear, my dear
in the mirror you shouldn't glare
Listen, hear me
The palpable wrinkles on your forehead
are the fragments of your unsung bygones
They're the graffitis of your amicable soul
that dance on everyone's heart
The glow in your burnt umber eyes
has been the moon of my dark nights
Once, twice, a hundred quivers
No wonder it's losing its fiery light!

Ahhh, those sunken lines around your eyes
voraciously flutter when you laugh
What if they only throb with unceasing frowns?
Oh, and your hair becoming wintry white
It's the crown of your bittersweet past
embellished with gems of grief and triumphs
Tell me, my love
will you barter
a map of a golden journey
an endless scroll of earned wisdom
An utmost metamorphosis
for a chalice of honey and nectar?
Tomorrow
when our hands are frail
our murmurs fail
Let the echoes of our melodies
douse the dulcet birds' chirps
Let our crisp memories
seep through the roots of weeping willow trees
Let our shriveled images
our palpable furrows
our gloomy eyes
our wintry white hair
evince in the autumn air
Let our hands, so frail
hold each other's tale
Let our murmurs steep
in ethereal silent weep
together with the sun sinking
in the horizon's deep

Secret Friend – Ken Anderson (he/him)

Smoke inflames his eyes
as loneliness will warp the way
he looks
at everything. He wonders
if he chose the part
he plays
or some blind impulse drives him here
at night
to blink
at noise and multicolored lights.

(A quiet stranger lights a fragrant joint, a secret friend
beside him
in the crowd.)

He watches numbers dancing
on a stage
like living puppets worked
by invisible strings. Then a show beguiles a room
of silhouettes
with guys made up
in drag, who dub the stars
and seem
to be
what they are not so well
he simply could not, if he cared to, tell.

(The quiet stranger offers him the joint.)

To Jesús – Ken Anderson (he/him)

I found an old memory
like a frayed photograph
in the back
of a drawer: you.

You told me
I could stay. Burnt
from a flame, I left a note: "Thanks."

One night, you stepped
into a diner
where I sipped black coffee
with my latest beau. We traded smiles, and I tried
to see
just what I hadn't loved.

You drifted
to a booth— we, a breakup.

This one loves that one,
and that one has it bad
for someone else. We draw a circle.

And when your dream now slyly plays your Spanish guitar,
I whisper, "Oh, amante, sí"

Bare Tierra – Jacob Teran (he/his/el)

I take off my shoes and squeeze my joints

I crunch them as I lay sitting upwards

The euphoria is spreading from the cranium down to tips of my toes

I want to hug my own body, but I do not know how to

    I take off my socks and glide my palms from my calves to my ankles

      I go back and forth as the sensation of touch electrifies my senses

                I then touch my feet

                 Bare with warmth

I squeeze my soles and interlace my fingers between my toes

I feel as if I am hugged

Loved

The power of touch

                 I hate
               having my
               feet touch
              the ground
                  bare

This particular moment I
slide my soles across the
ground

The desolate earth I can feel beneath my feet

The sun shining above is my blanket and warms my chest and back

I crunch my toes picking up conglomerates
of dirt and minerals

The tierra embraces me

I lay down half bare hugging the earth as it

Embraces me back

I am learning how to love and hug myself.

Mi Color – Jacob Teran (he/his/el)

Un Chicano comes in different colors

Mine is Brown

I was taught to not love my color

I was told that my color resembles mierda

I believed that my color was not of Indigenous

It was not until I grew older that I saw that my color is beautiful

Envied and hated by some

Kissed by the sun itself

Simon que si!

I was born in the Estados Unidos, not Mexico, but I feel a link to my
Mexican Ancestry

Some Indigenous Identity that I do not recall when I look in the
mirror

But I see someone that is familiar

I cannot name him, but I feel I have seen him before

I am searching to further fortify my Indigenous Roots of whence I
came

I am seeking to fully embrace the identity of where I fit in this world

The seeds of my Roots have been planted but not nourished

Dwindled but not withered

Awoken after a long slumber

To embrace the color of my Indigenous Plants is a love long awaited

To belong to La Tierra, my own home

How much have my Indigenous Plants grown

Brown and strong

With love and pride do my Indigenous Plants grow more

Slow Life – Nicholas Olah (he/him)

The branches are still
for the first time
this month.

The grass, dusted with frost,
glistens like a star-
filled sky.

A light rain begins to fall
and it is the only
sound.

Soft – Nicholas Olah (he/him)

On this day, I am awoken by
a symphony of birds singing hallelujah
just outside my bedroom window.

Later, my niece curls into a U-shape against
my ribcage and every corner of me
that can love splits open.

Indeed:
in some ways,
the world is still soft.

Stealing Time/Entanglement – Karen Arredondo (she/they)

To unglue would mean to tangle up In a war with myself/
At the possibilities and potential
I am forced to choose a path
Steer, veer, fearing
A wrong turn and I'll lose…. myself.
One blood
Our blood fused.
One life
We choose
Who might take on paths towards
Enlightenment,
Entanglement
Together wasn't guaranteed
Enchanted by the idea that time is what we make of it
We always took advantage—
My feelings towards a certain thing or humans are
Just a side effect of what tangled strings provided
When you couldn't—
For connection if we let it
Get to the best sides of us,
I bet it's like knowing yourself
Seeing the best sides of you or the worst
Through time,
Elasticity
Tensile strength tug and release
Reflect.
Am I easy to let go of, forgettable,
Tangible no longer wanted
The least effect
Of change

When I see a reflection of the same time
I see I am powerful, dangerous, fearless and kind.
To admit that it wasn't right
Okay, it wasn't right for now. It felt right then, and was right for a
long while/
Until it wasn't.
What affects us both
Better choices you denied yourself come from the tangled up
thoughts pulling you away from
Peaceful stances
Release the fact
That things don't turn out as you planned
Let go.
Forget what hurts
I forgot what hurt.
Beget
Bygones
Upset
It's right
I can't let it get the best of me
I keep saying these things
TIme to reflect
I am better off
I am better off
I am better off
I am better off.

We are better off
I will love you forever
To see you happy
Makes all the hurt good.

Nervous systems – Karen Arredondo (she/they)

Hold man's breath
Holds tightening
Held back
Background blurred
Shallow rise and fall of his chest
Eye sees shadows
Blocked dulled pain slows down
Nervous systems
Navigation through
Heights and center parked stimulations.
Overall
Drive
Increased
Peaked
Pain
Surged
Pinched
Dulled
Severed or burned
Removed
Numbed.
Nervous systems
Existence
Meant to ride
Protection
Feels
Present
Hyper vigilant

Tricks the brain
Into feeling things dreamt up
Imagined
Faked
Taken for reality
Mistaken
Defense mechanisms

an imaginary sheet – Lucía Retta (she/her)

of glass
of sky
of uncertain memories
gently draped over the divide, like—
how the cold lives on your skin, like—
how i saw you in the distance &
you offered the empty expanse of your skin
the dark fruit of your heart
the weight of your hand
your simple dreams
your unending desires

how difficult you are to carry, yet
how gently your wrist grazed mine

(here i left an offering)

(in variations   recalibrations   accumulations)

i am waiting for your eyes to meet mine.

weathered, variegated, spare – Lucía Retta (she/her)

*"and the world will come from your mouth, escaping through the
window like a river"*
—Alexandro Jodorowsky

i cannot read your limit
is it constant, mapped, marked, or—
undone, tangled, trestled by desire lines
we walk a path we made
beside all we wished to forget
fallen trees, roots exposed
streams running lower this year
burn scars across the meadow
all of the past that marks us

have you been lost, or—
simply unobserved for so long

together we walk an old passage
rough with rocks newly exposed
by a fresh snowmelt
a new burn

don't trip, you tell me, don't trip
<blockquote>and the sky was empty
and the tender line of the horizon
shifted with every move</blockquote>
don't trip
<blockquote>out in the open at last, in the field
i angled toward your heart, a harvest
and me, a knife</blockquote>

and i want you with my sharp edges
            but we cannot hold the same weapon
            one of us must take the handle
            and one of us must hold the blade
                              the curve of memory
                              all that floods
                              all that floats
                              and the blood drip

and we melt into each other over decades, over decades.

Directions Home – M.F. (they/she)

Ink stains the paper,
at last,
They leave,
suspended in rhythm.
2 years consumed aspiration,
but longing
was not so easily digested.
Creatures woven together like cloth,
Only gods' hands
trembled. Leaving knots
that swelled like a bruise.
Pieces quietly collected, gently
swept into the dustpan
by those too small
to hold the broom.
The walls whisper *"What have we done?"*
Locked doors weep, Christmas lights melt snow,
Their indigo blanket has holes in it.
Forgiveness had a certain sweetness,
but overindulgence left the tongue sore. Drunk yourself sick again,
From swallowing too much of the sunset.
Years of ache collect dust on the mantle.
Neatly untouched, framed
and displayed to all.
It bleeds through the decade.
Nurtured fruit blooms on a once lonely tree.
The moon walks with Them
around the lake.
Somewhere,
They are in love.

Everyone's father cheated on their mother, but mine truly loved her.
he learned the intricacies of her being, plotting the map of her soul.
he traced the curves and the scars on her torso, he memorized the
lines on her face. And he would strike, the way you strike a match on
your blue jeans, faded and ready for friction. Everyone's father cheated
on their mother, but mine couldn't stop.
Even when yesterday's leftover grease congealed, and the vacuum
stopped working. Even when the eagles and bears from home called to
him. The rhubarb from the campari was simply too good, too warm,
too comforting.
Like a friend softly whispering *"take all you need."*
Everyone's father cheated on their mother,
but mine never stopped.
Not even when little hands collected bottles from his feet,
found emails on his computer, or took
Her face in their little hands and held Her while she shook.
Home was hidden, hidden from him,
and he never knew it.
he still does not know it.
Everyone's father cheated on their mother,
but mine will never know it.

**Note: Nôhtâwiy means my father in Plains Cree.*

Apology to the Moon Goddess – Sara Wiser (she/her/hers)

Diana,
I hate that name.
I know who you really are.

Artemis.
My goddess.
My huntress.
My moon mother.

I promised you when I was a child to always look up at the stars.
I promised you that I would remain forever wild,
unable to be tamed,
chaste,
pure,
untouched.

But
I love love.
I love to be loved,
I love to feel the joys of skin on mine.

Can we come to an agreement?
That loving is holy,
that loving is worship
to you,

to the moon.

My Selene,
is he not Endymion?
The reincarnation of your half-love?

Orion guards the skies,
the other half lover.

I am aching to have let you down.
Maybe I'm just weak,
maybe I'm just a hopeless romantic.
Maybe I'm just a girl
who has been raised like they told her to be.

Or maybe,
just maybe,
I can carry it all within me.

And maybe
I can contain these infinities.

Broken? – Chris Dorian (he/him)
CW: mental health & suicidal ideations

We exist in dimly lit, dingy, small rooms with painted block walls or
some 2020 version of 70s wood paneling
Surrounded by wires, and machines, and monitors, and pseudo-
concerned individuals asking if you have not just a plan but means
Then we transition to cozy couches, zen gardens, and inspirational
quotes for about an hour at a time, talking about all the terrible shit
in our lives
Struggling with how sad or suicidal we really are if the only thing
stopping the finality of death being our worry about how others
would be impacted
But we know this is not life
Or at least how we should exist
"Have you tried live, laugh, love" someone asks, because Facebook
told them to
We've probably tried it all, short of recharging our vitality by
sunning our assholes in the great wide open, turning our rears to
the sun
Well, some might have even done that
Tried everything, maybe even the drugs
Not the fun kind (but we've tried them too)
The prescribed meds
But only to stop or doubt the reward
I mean, at the end of the day, we still want to feel
To not be numb or blunted
And we want our dicks to still work
Put us in nature
Pound some drums and let us feel bass in our soles and souls
Be an ear
Be a shoulder
Be a presence
Just don't be an asshole who tells me we are lucky, we are

privileged enough to be sad about shit because others have it
worse, and we would get better if we did something for ourselves
and thought happy thoughts.
Let us express ourselves without it being perceived as hostility
Or weakness
Or being pussies who can't "man up"
I cried today
I'll cry again
Maybe even before lunch
Don't look away or dismiss
Hand me a tissue
Better yet, keep the box for yourself and let me let them flow
proudly
Just don't expect any of this to actually cure or fix us
WE. ARE. NOT. BROKEN.
We just aren't our best selves right now
But we are getting there
And if the product has some cracks, we embrace it
It gives us character
It gives us history
It gives us hope because if we sealed them once before we can
again
We ask you don't walk for us
Walk with us
Walk away from us
Just don't get in the fucking way

Love Language – Chris Dorian (he/him)

I know how to love and love one way only
Doting
Overbearing
In your face
Serving you
Carry you along the way
Love
It's annoying, I know, but it's my love
And I cannot lower the volume or turn it off
Maybe it's a love language I never received
Maybe it's a love language I developed waking up next to someone,
seeing them, and talking with them every day for a quarter of my
life
Maybe it's a love language fueled by years of insecurity and
rejection
Maybe it's a love language that's really been there all along,
embedded from childhood
Maybe it's because when I find something, someone, I like
I want
I love
I enter into that with every ounce of energy and of passion I have in
each of my starstuff molecules
(Hell, check my sign if you're into that sort of thing)
When someone is hurting, I give more
When someone is in need, I give more
And when that passion and love is not enough, I give more
I. Do. Not. Know. Another. Way.
And that is unfortunate
Because I always find myself left empty
Alone
And without any love left to give myself

Lupercal – Laura Jane Round (she/they)

They suckle at me
Though I long to stay
Near the chunks of flesh.
My pack flay with teeth,
Tongues.
The male, with tongue of fire
Nips at bellies and has first taste.
A waste
I think when his mate did the slaying
While he slunk in the shadows, feigned fatigue.

My boys are strange.
Furless save for their sweet heads.
They yowl at night like wounded prey
But I am soft and yielding
They take comfort in my thick pelt
Small cries like whispers in my back,
Like the hunter's knife.
I will absorb
What they cannot stand.

Malfunctioning – Steve Denehan (he/him)

It is Tuesday
or Wednesday
I move from room to room
a pilot
in a malfunctioning machine
the morning mist
has dissipated
leaving a sheen on the grass
it looks new
but it is not
it Is as old as the hills
the bog
the silver birch
the water that has pooled
beneath the leaking gutter
I find myself in the kitchen
things swirl into focus
it is Wednesday
I am sure
that it is Wednesday

JAN 17 // WAS I ONE OF YOUR NEW YEAR'S RESOLUTIONS? –
Cassandra Traina (she/her/hers)

Sit and watch our breath smoke the air as though we are children and
this is just the morning.
This is just one morning in many mornings that
we will never remember for the simplicity of it.
Sit and quarter our lives, this piece: family,
this piece: friendship, this piece: romance, this piece: acquaintances.
Yes, that about does it.
That makes it all even, parsed out, and faceable.
But what of strangers—their cool presence in the periphery of our
lives?
What of *you,* who is making a slow, but irreversible movement to the
periphery?
What of blame?
I know you well, but not as well as I used to.
You are proof of the way beauty can be put away and never used.
The opening of a lip is too much like the closing of a door
to be anything more than a passage through which we move our kept
meanings.
I am waiting for your next movement through the space between us.
All the multitudes of space between us.
I want you to know that you were reckless with this, whatever this was.

We're all mourning over the remnants of who we were to each other.

Let it inform you.
Let it make the form of you.
Half processed, the other half raw and slathered—butter.
Yes, like the richness of butter.
Like the sweetness too, sweet from the gleaming morning of land. Full
and not from the market, but from the hands,
which came from the market first anyways.
Let it veil you, but not for too long:
do not be hidden for too long.
Fill the lade and move out, move into the approach of a force greater
than yours.
Fill another body than your own with tempered care
and let the overflowing happen.

FEB 21 // CREATURES – Cassandra Traina (she/her/hers)

I would make a fantastic duck.
It's not so glamorous, but I would.
I really would make a great duck.
I'd be clean and neat and—now that I think about it, I'd make a good
fox too.

And by fox I mean—a small mouth.
And by small mouth I mean pry it open with your "fuck me" hands.
I *mean* I want to be pried open. Or curled shut? Yes, curled shut.
Like a winter-tired fox sleeping in the corner of some wood, drawn to
its own warmth.

I would make a brilliant snowflake and I would take comfort
in my place amongst the millions. Small fish in a big sea and all.
I would feel relief in my swarm of communal, radical beauty.
I wouldn't even have to be the perfect example of a snowflake to be
happy.

I would make a comfortable world for myself—
if only I were left to my own morph-tations.
And sometimes, I think I would make a beautiful lover in any body but
this. With any lover but him.

FEB 26 // SNOW MOON – Cassandra Traina (she/her/hers)

I like looking into the gray-lit windows of bogus houses on my walks.
Men at computers and women at counters, children everywhere.

A man on the corner is leaning out of his bathroom window
with a detachable showerhead, dulling the sharp icicles
leached onto his doorway with its hot torrent.
He sends the bodied water rushing down the hill
to meet the coursing stream below the concrete.

The blue and orange of the sky and streetlight reflect on the snow.
Everything is bright and imperfect in the damp light of the snow moon.
The extended hand of winter's God is getting more abused every day.
Blackened by low cars leaving clotted clouds—their compressed speed
and scraped filth.
Dog prints, dog shit in the snow.

I track myself through the hamlet; through familiar nuclear courses.
Still, it changes, the self-imposed nature of it.

MARCH 7 // SLEEPY REMEMBRANCE – Cassandra Traina
(she/her/hers)

Remember when sheer tights were worth the itchy winter thighs,
the quick friction of bloated hands needed
to defrost the fat beneath the tunneled plumage?
Remember when a tongue-pinked lip, a symbol of premature sex
and directed invitation was a natural kind of gesture?
And crossing and uncrossing your legs was the feminine mathematic:
adding up, catching, a little bit of releasing, and finally possession.
This is all to say that I thought I knew what I wanted,
and I was very good at setting my sights on it.
When I was seven, I was burdened with the idea that the sky would fall.
When I turned seventeen, I was sure of it, and that only made me want
a baby more.
I don't want a child as much as I did then; with the feverish obsession
of loving a small being.
I want a child, only not for the same reasons—I don't think it'll ever be
for those reasons again.

This Will Be Done Very Sensitively As Isabel Does Not Like To Be Seen As Different – Isabel de Silva (she/her)

This is what I get for always being the dog.
Part of the family but removed from it.
Left subservient and waiting for everyone else to come home.

When my sister was a baby I fed her avocados and in return she made me an animal.
Assigned Canine By Sister.
A role to make me a part of the game by any means necessary.

I have carried those dogs with me.
We cower from fireworks and yearn to be a part of the bigger picture.
Wandering downstairs for attention when we're bored.

An insistence from loved ones to go outside and take part when all I really want to do is sit by the fire and listen.

If Keats ate Toast – Emma Conally-Barklem (she/her)

Winter bear with me

     as I lurch in stunned lethargy

through glacial fragments of

     an ice flower soul.

Shards sting crisp,

     a February sorbet

tang of recollection,

     bury me threefold in

toast, butter and jam,

     a predilection

to hibernate beneath

     ivy leaf.

A snow drake's down

     to cleave my heart rate

five fathoms down.

The Smallest Church in the Country – Emma Conally-Barklem
(she/her)

The smallest church in the country is planted in Upleatham;
Rough-hewn, cornice drifts encase beatitudes in frigid glazed air.
Lone egg yolk tealight with bitter wick stands sentinel.

Gingerbread house picture perfect, enclosed by Yew trees and Lung
wort
Quaint eighteenth-century carvings of moon-faced angels,
Frosted stain glass windows,
As winter's benevolence reveals,
Deer tracks and mole uprisings.

An arcadia nativity of creatures
Hushed, secretive, snow-packed
Slanted Solstice December light
In this hallowed grove, on Wintertide,
The season sighs ennui

The Search of the Angry Breeze – Kenneth Stephens (he/him)

Only the moss now moves my tongue,
though I crossed streams and climbed
ridges and walked the lonely trails.
Only the moss under the melting snow.

Only the fire now moves my soul,
though I would hear in the night
the search of the angry breeze.
Only the fire and the fallen trees.

In Essence – A. Bhardwaj (she/her)

My eyes are forced open by harsh, bright rays
and the outside, cloaked in soft snow
humanity's sharp geometric edges rounded by the lull of the world

Outside exists year-round in the corners of my mind
stacked neatly next to sleeping memories
preserved in ice

That first step in the frigid morning
Leaning into your door, the force of a person cracks the miniature
mountain range
Cementing your home shut

Light dances off the undisturbed plane of suburbia
and for a moment, hung moonlike in liminal time
you exist alone in the world
silence muffles the soft thrum of your heart

Tilting your chin back, the wind sears the space between
Worn woolen scarf and the downturn of your lips
catching glimpses of long ago on your tongue
gone faster than blinks

Your eyes are bound by the crystallizing frost
Forcing them open, you search the monochrome sky
Dizzying and vast, a dreamscape you cannot ink into words
Lost adrift in the spiral of snow

You begin to descend
deeper, into warm quilts, patched and repatched through the
seasons
oak piled high, as dancing flames chase creeping frost away
and in your slumber, you dream of white swaths and wind-chapped
cheeks

Outage: a winter storm haibun – Daniella Navarro (she/her)

Hibernation, it seems. So frozen yet sweating under all of the blankets I own. The last warm thing I ate, I don't even remember, but I know I didn't squirrel away any of the heat for later—for now. Subsisting off of Gateau d' Amour, a perk of enjoying our anniversary just yesterday. Sick already of Gateau d' Amour. There's a metaphor in there somewhere.

Without power and water—
how thin this tether is
between us and small comforts

inheritance – Daniella Navarro (she/her)

Your last Thanksgiving, we celebrated
weeks early so we could celebrate at all.

You couldn't keep anything down, but maybe a bite
or two of the banana cream pie you requested I bake.

Our nieces' and nephews' inheritances
doled out from your bed.

A figurine, a jersey, anything
to be remembered.

James was the only one
who cried. "Say hi to my dad for me."

Cancer has taken so much
from this family and given nothing
but sorrow in return. Maybe

that is just our inheritance.

hell – Daniella Navarro (she/her)

is reading the poems I wrote before you died. It is knowing
I buried their author sometime after
I collapsed by your graveside, playing

the one song Trisha didn't include in your rosary slideshow, but before
our great aunt carried me away. It is having to Google your smile,

your laugh. It is being Judas to my own skin. It is sitting comfort-
less while the priest tells our parents that their only begotten son died

at the same age Jesus was predicted to have been. It is the certainty
that one day I will be older than God. It is seeing every moan make me

smaller. It is every heartbreak, all this grief, tearing off pieces
of myself until I am nothing but moons. I have limbs that miss

their sockets and a chest that misses its heart. It is thinking that love
feels like a funeral. It is love and war existing

as synonyms. It is soulmates dying at 15. It is rearranging the words
in this poem and coming up with the same damn thing. Hell

is November. November is being broken up with while on break
at work. Returning to answering phone calls

and handing out dressing room numbers like my heart isn't lusting
for air. November is a willingness to give up everything to feel

that type of alive again, unaware in the bliss of an inconsequential
dress rehearsal. It is replaying your death over and over again until

I can't measure my stare in yards. It is being scared
I would never be able to forget the sound you made when you died,

and being right. It is my psychologist calling it PTSD, knowing
I only went to war with my memory. My life
is a string of perpetual Novembers.

ofrenda – Daniella Navarro (she/her)

Thinking of what I could offer you, brother now to dirt and a cemetery of bodies. You passed just shy of 34. The same age as Jesus, the priest noted in your eulogy. Our father's only begotten son sacrificed for something I can't seem to articulate.

Your first "official" Dia de los Muertos, we gathered at your gravesite. Mom made you a tray of enchiladas. Cheese, your favorite. We buried a pair near your headstone and beckoned your spirit to rise again in fulfillment of the Scriptures.

In that moment, I imagined you were the ants scurrying past our feet.

Stone by Stone – Meghan King (she/her)

Once I was drowning in anxiety and depression
A depth of darkness of which I didn't see a way out
Sitting at the bottom of a well, dragging myself out of the sediment
Reaching and clinging to the mossy walls for leverage
Climbing slowly, willfully, stone by stone, scraping my palms
Anguish, a reminder to not grow weary, to fight for freedom
Strength with each calloused scar
Hope, a shining beacon into the cavernous dark
I imagined peace and new beginnings.
As my hand reached over the edge of the well, urged onward by an unseen warmth
Reassurance in a future of joy and purpose

Love in Brooklyn – Meghan King (she/her)

Proud and honorable
That's what your walk proclaims
Yet life has you feeling defeated

You may feel shame, but damn
You're not the same man
The man strolling Kew Gardens
Demanding respect, fighting for your place

I come alive in Brooklyn
That's where I see you
You may be from Queens
But, damn, I see you everywhere

The waves crash off Surf Ave
The wind carries chili fries and hotdogs
Us sitting under an umbrella
Concrete tables, us laughing
The waves crash and sing our melody
I see you in the sea glass and shells I collect
I hear you in the crowds on rides
The carnival music and Edison lights

I'd walk 3rd Avenue with you
Mi corazon es tuyo, estoy pensando
Lo siento, pero estoy aqui.
I walk past the Brownstones
The Brooklyn Bridge smiles at us

Bookmark Shoppe and cafes, my favorite stops
I imagine what it'd be like holding your hand as I browse the newest
local poets

I want you next to me
Strolling into a bar, Margheritas my favorite
You have a beer, chilled and glistening
As I sip my salted glass, you tilt the bottle to your lips
Oh, how I wish to kiss those lips.
For you to reach out your hand to enfold mine
Pero estoy solamente pensando.

Haunted – Meghan King (she/her)

I am haunted by our memories.
Of what I had envisioned for us.
The promises and life I had believed you wanted too.
Haunted by your laughter
Haunted by your smile
Haunted needing to catch my breath when our eyes would meet
Haunted memories of a connection; acceptance I'd never known
Haunted entwined souls and hearts
Haunted still seeing my delicate hand in yours

Liturgy For Good Girls – Elizabeth Core Shenk (she/her)

If you want to herd the devil,
let the flowers in the sidewalk grow.
If you want him wearing wool,
running scared over cliffs,
hang something scandalous
on the clothing line.
Be less fearsome,
and fear a little less—
Live like a living human,
dance and swear
eat butter, have sex,
say what you really think.
The trick is
to eat when you're hungry
and scratch when you itch
and sing when you're happy
and scream and flail and roar
when you're sad or angry.
(See, darkness has you where he wants you
when you live your human life
like you're nothing but a dirty god.)
And then,
after all of this living,
keep loving
the wild oddness—
the impossibility—
of you being here
for just the briefest moment
in this messy and haunting and holy world.

Longing, Maybe? – Elizabeth Core Shenk (she/her)

I wish there was a word
for the way a body feels
when day begins to fold
into twilight.

It's the same as
the first time it rains
in September.

It's the same as
when you're alone.

It's something like
the taste of metal.

It's something like
being far from home.

Kid Smile – Elizabeth Core Shenk (she/her)

I love the way joy looks
when it hides behind the corners
of your mouth.
The way you're cupping your smile
like a lightning bug trapped under your hands.
I can still see your happiness flicker,
you know,
I can still see it dance.

**burning haibun - ice bathing –
Mirjam Mahler** (she/her)

I **tried ice bathing** in a cold lake
for the first time on a January
morning because I wanted to
write a poem about an
adventure. I had been thinking
about the prompt for a few
days, but there were no new
adventures in my life and I
didn't want to write about
something from half a decade
ago.

The lake was partially frozen
and the air temperature was
just slightly above freezing. I
joined a group of experienced
ice bathers and we did some
warming up exercises and
guided breathwork. Since the
group was quite large not
everyone could go in at the
same time and I had to wait my
turn. As soon as I stepped into
the lake the cold **took my
breath** away. A friend with
more ice bathing experience
noticed and commended
"Breathe! Breathe! Breathe!".
The cold felt incredibly painful. I
could not relax into the feeling
at all. After a few minutes I fled,
searching for warmth but it took
me a long time to get dressed
with my frozen clumsy fingers. I

felt the **cold lingering** in my
bones **all day**. This had been
something to try, an adventure,
but **not** something I felt like
repeating or turning into a
habit.

I go swimming in lakes all
summer long but didn't **return**
to that lake until the first days
of fall when it was still quite
warm. The ice bathing group
had continued being active and I
decided to join them again after
I had been ignoring their
messages all year. I liked the
idea of being a person who does
ice bathing just like I liked the
idea of being a person who does
yoga or triathlons. This time the
warming up exercise felt like a
bit of a joke, the water was
warm and I ended up going for a
long swim. From then on I
returned almost every Sunday.

October had been unusually
warm and getting into the lake
was not really a challenge. I
learned to **let go.** As I stepped
into the water I had a **vision.** I
have a photo of my
grandmother as a young girl in a
bathing suit with short hair and
a fresh face and a look full of
confidence and I felt her next to
me **cheering** me on.

I can do this.
The next Sunday I was filmed slowly emerging from the water, calmly picking the seaweed off my shoulders. I looked so **calm** and content.

Since the twenty minute drive to the lake seemed a bit of a waste for the few minutes I spent in the water I **added** a **morning run** along the river before the dip and I listened to audiobooks while I greeted the ducks, swans and even an occasional heron.

I enjoyed these excursion, the transition from **movement to stillness**.

On the first Sunday in November I drove to the lake in a foggy cloud and could hardly see the river on my run.

This time the group of ice bathers was quite large and introductions and explanations took a long time. By the time we undressed I was freezing, the sweat on my skin now making the cold almost unbearable.

As the big group walked towards the water I went off to the side and found my own private space and an unhindered view of the foggy surface. This time the water felt much colder, but as the **liquid embraced** me and I watched the **ripples** from my body on the water's **surface** I felt **greeted**.

You have arrived.

What started as an adventure is emerging into a new way of experiencing nature and my body.

tried
ice bathing
took my breath
cold lingering all day
not

return
let go
vision grandmother cheering
I can do this
calm

added
morning run
movement to stillness
liquid embraces, ripples surface
greeted

ice bathing took breath
let go, movement to stillness
liquid embraces

ice bathing haiku - yearn for adventure

yearn for adventure
took a dip in frozen lake
overcame with pride

ice bathing elfchen - emerge

emerge
cold liquid
infusing calm energy
melting away hot anxiety
renewed

ice bathing haiku - going to the lake

going to the lake
dip into the cold liquid
meditation heat

Paper Flowers – Emilija Veljković (she/her)

Anya sat by the river every day, watching the clear water flow on its own, traveling through the quiet valley. The sky was cloudless, the gentle spring breeze playing with the strands of Anya's hair.

Anya came to this secret place of hers, always bringing a bag with her. She took out the pieces of paper from the bag: red, purple, orange, pink, and yellow. There was no particular reason behind the choice; Anya just liked the colors.

Anya made flowers out of the paper she brought with her. Anya enjoyed her solitude, folding the paper gently to resemble a flower shape.

Anya's mother taught her how to fold the paper into the beautiful shape of a flower. It was a delicate process that required concentration and patience.

"It doesn't matter if you try and fail." The most important thing is the effort you put forth. The results will come gradually," is what Anya's mother used to say to her when she was frustrated about not folding the paper right.

"But, mom, what if I never get it right?" Anya didn't want to disappoint her mother who always took the time to sit with her and play with paper.

"Oh, honey, don't worry No matter how long it takes, I'm sure you'll do it. And even if you don't, that won't change anything. I'll always love you and support you; remember that."

Anya returned to the present. Those memories resurface when she's by the river, making paper flowers. It seemed like an eternity since Anya first started this little hobby of hers.

No, not a hobby. It was a ritual that she shared with her mother—an unspoken promise made between a mother and a daughter.

It was the only thing left that still connected Anya to her mother.

She never gave up making paper flowers, even in the toughest of times.

The paper flowers that she let float on the water's surface were Anya's way to feel close to someone dear to her—to someone who was no longer physically there.

However, her mother's gentle touch guides Anya even now as she sits by the river in her own little world.

Anya's mother is there, in those paper flowers that Anya so lovingly creates.

Melancholia – Dani Solace (they/he/she)

Sitting in an ocean of my tears,
everything seems so small.
I don't mean to be harsh,
but I am heavy-handed at heart.
Wide and tall and clumsy and so *much*
it is suffocating.
I am suffocating.

These endless, empty waters offer no solace.
All that stares back at me
Is my reflection,
rippling with pity.

Is there something wrong with me? – Dani Solace (they/he/she)

Though I'm in no rush to leave you,
nothing pulls me to stay.
I'm at ease
and for some reason
so far away.
Is there a flaw in my system?
I want, *need*, to feel something.
Instead, I sit on the edge
unable to push myself one way or the other.
Unable to give what you're asking for.

Whether my heart is in this frozen ground
or the hands of the man I thought of all night long
I'll never say.
Perhaps I'm prolonging the inevitable
with my questionable ways
but I cannot help my distaste
with both intimacy
and monogamy.
Is there something so wrong
with loving everyone all at once?

Sirens' Song – Dani Solace (they/he/she)

Does it frighten you when my thunder shakes the earth?
Those nauseating cries for release
resounding with a force that melts your brain
until it drips
slowly
out of your ears.

Is it alarming when I take up space?
Unrestrained and unashamed,
I shatter the paradise you built for yourself
taking every bit of life with me
to decompose
In the sand below.
Is that why you're worlds away?
Am I too much?

It's easy to be enchanted by pretty things.
I know that's why you always come back to me.
Even when violence haunts your dreams,
you cannot look away.
Caught up in a coral haze,
lost in a serpentine gaze.
Will you love me until the end of days?

This may be your last if you come any closer.
The winds will not spare you
and they only grow colder.
Do you feel it in your bones yet?
The sun won't touch where I'm from.
There is no mercy here.
The steel that embraces me may glimmer in the moonlight
but it *will* bite.

The Husking Hour – K Weber (she/her)

In my boots I have traveled to warm and unravel
the frozen birch-bark among
the risk of icicles.

In my mittens I peel a secret message from tree's
skin; fumbling as I would with the rind
of an impatient orange.

In my mind the smell of cinnamon and clove
simmers while my knitted hat sweats
at the forehead as I find fortune.

The Gardeners Sleep In – R.H. Alexander (he/him)

This morning has trees
rimed of diamond frost
to gift the end
of the gardens.
Say autumn is here.
Say marry me.
We don't care.

We'd rather be freshly planted,
wet skin on wet skin softened
by the weightlessness of pleasure,
when it's complete exhaustion and on top
of it all more hunger
more heat, more rain, more sun.

Awake let's find
something you were.
The way our arms held.
How the weeding does.

After You Said I Love You – R.H. Alexander (he/him)

How it was to stand
in the water for hours,
herons claiming minnows,
knowing their little hearts
like you knew mine.

Shore reeds tell the wind
their reasons, rasp out the dreams
waiting in our throat.
If it was this clear,
I would have said it long ago.

She With the Gift Sees the Dead – R.H. Alexander (he/him)

She with the gift sees the dead
come and go, follow along.
We bring hope to our private viewings,
walk throughs, consider kitchens
the aging furnace, the longish drives to town,
how much time we have.

Not this one, she says, pointing out
a little girl in the corner of the dark study,
a ragged angel all done in white.
This one's eyes have been taken,
can't see us but knows we are here,
says she with the gift.

Out the door we go
walk away from house number forty-three
looked at and walked through
and walked away from them all
because she with the gift dismembers disbelief,
all those creaks and groans keeping you up at night.
All the old houses come with them,
the bare whimpered sighs
the little ones give
to remember them by.
She with the gift tells me so.

She with the gift finds the reasons
to say no. Our agent is so patient.
I will work with you until we find the right one,
she says, the one with no gift but her own truth
no matter the winking bulb in the bathroom,
the first midnight knock at the door.

Hopeless Naivety – Evan Violets (he/him)
for those caught in unrequited love.

we started structuring (seemingly feasible)
possibility from the impossibilities.
the sudden onset of selective courage is inexplicable.
the unrequited nature of things would
surface occasionally in the multitude of
reasons.   your midnight assurances
transit into my internal anthem...
your un-smudging aura, unrivalled vibrancy.
your eyes tell a multitude of tales with their incandescence.
(and part of me realises you might never understand that...)

      although i amplified my holler arcing around
      you...*although* i yelled with every last ounce
      of longing left in my lungs (into the
      distance)...*although* i extended, tried incessantly
      to reiterate my sentiments to you
      (in the most thoughtless of actionable ways),
      i couldn't reach you.
      i thought I'd inched forward enough, so
      i called out to you but—

      i couldn't reach you

An Inventory of Things / People Blooming Mean to Me – Evan Violets (he/him)

i.   transitional process, picking up the shattered
gradations of our imploded solace with our callous-spangled
fingers and piecing them into unfamiliar
kinds of brilliance.

ii.   the lengths we've come, to comprehend the ways to
bend our lingering agonies into ocean-tender art.

iii.   the dusk-shrouded days we've trudged past,
to be able to warp our dismal silhouette(s)
into tangible lustre.

iv.   the way the static skyline transits into sunset
aftermath, the way its cerulean softness
blossomed into raw-apricot scenery.

v.   the way we waltzed out of the perpetual winter
littered in our marrows, the way we spite the gates
that'd once entrapped us with their arctic ribs.

vi.   the way we excavate the solemnities scarring within

vii.   the way we discard the whispers encumbering our dreams
(although they'd always come back)

viii.   and you, grandma, the way you grew out of your
episodic-grieving, into a figure of incandescence,
inspiring those around you.

We Paint This Turbulence in Hues – Evan Violets (he/him)
for someone in my past, turbulence is okay...

our stories remain tainted with the tragedies
we've lived to reminisce.   the columns
of unwaning gale, regressing with age.
they still usher us into baltic lamentations for all
we've lived to lose.   our loss, leaving evident
void of what our tomorrows would be
scented in...   our loss,
undisputed wreckage in the chest.   (the same chest
vested with all the greyest emotions our
kindergartens never taught us how to decipher)

colour blending, (or so we were taught,) wasn't
the most practical thing in our contexts. the
ravaged reserves of grime-clothed-gloom
never materialised into anything worth the effort,
ever.   our despondence   and
our strangest of shadow shapes and tinges were
destined for an existence synonymous only
to ruining (and wounding) the most magnificent
things.

they said they wanted literature eased of weeping
and nightmare-nouns, they wanted literature that'd
embodied something more than what had already
been said.

but i guess we will keep painting our turbulence in hues...
we will keep painting this turbulence in hues...

Ever-Pondering Him – Evan Violets (he/him)

he calls truancy a symptom of existential
crisis and he calls sadness an extension
of her fingertips. he held in his blistered
hand a handful of dreams,

dreams in which his anguish would thaw
under the moonlight, dreams in which his
longing knew of summer's embrace,
dreams in which his blueness is translatable,
malleable, tangible, salvageable, dreams
in which, his inability to hope would unravel
its existence, and melt into a puddle of
nothing at all.

he refers to the recurring pop culture
themed in the genres of a fading yellow—
as apt metaphor for the bitter truth that'd
never made a clear debut apart from the
everyday headlines.   he plots out strategy
to flush out the sourness of the surrounding air,
unknowing of the sourness that emerged as
psychological remnant of the unaddressed loopholes.

he contemplates the weight of ghosting as
incomprehensible something wavering in
the atmosphere, an ambience of possible
danger, yet he'd generally grown into
a state of chronic numbness regarding it,
with time, steadily, *with time.*

We Used to Be So Soft – Evan Violets (he/him)
For Emily

you said *life can't survive without chaos*
it'd go on, send a barrage of disorganised sensations
down the lengths of my spine.   we're such an
ominously seamless representation of the roughening
effects time has on the soul (or virtually, anything...)

you asked *when you grow out of your childlike state,
who greets you in the "real world"?*   and i was
genuinely tangled in a state of rapid conceptually
conception.   but i would soon settle for the ~~plain~~
hypernym "disappointment" was. even with every fabric
of imagery laid bare,   they'd never begin
to express a strand of bitterness we'd feel.

i illustrated this colossal wave of unmeasured heft in a
relatively lacklustre manner.   truth was...
i wasn't even the slightest bit ready to shoulder the weight
of this tidal language, this sweeping motion of reality,
i wasn't even ready for the impending wind-knocking
sucker-punches served by the unscheduled change surfacing.

we'd never truly graduate from our phases of uncertainty,
the deliberations of dreams and feasibilities.
these occurrences of intuition, how'd they define the footsteps
unplanted? would we stray in the event of shrouding hope?   *no,
we couldn't.*   would we lose sight of art?   *no, we can't.* would
we surrender our dreams to the reality checks knocking
rhythmically at our conscience?   *no, we mustn't.*

b's and d's – Laura Beth Johnson (she/her)

The truth is I have trouble with my b's and d's
Last week I wrote bebuctive
I've texted I need to go to ded plenty of times

C'mon you say, it's just one line and a circle
Well sometimes the circle goes on the right, sometimes on the left
And I happen to mix up my lefts and rights

Right here on the left my Uder passenger says
which is already confusing so I'd hold out
my pointer fingers on the wheel to see which one made an L

L's I bon't have problems with.
L is a perpendicular situation.
Though I suppose so is T and I've never written Tamp instead of
Lamp

Uppercase B is alright. Same with uppercase D
even though they're only
a line through the middle bifferent

It's a wonder we get any of these letters right
They're just lines and circles
and bots

2 Atlingworth Street – Laura Beth Johnson (she/her)

There was a pharmacy on the corner
of the bedside table
motion sickness pills for the train
a bottle of tiny moons for my depression

In the closet was the market
patterned scarves on six white hangers
street corners colored with flags
from countries we had never heard of
and a clothing store for men and women, our sizes

A grocery bustled in the fridge
ketchup on the ledge, gouda in the cheese drawer
silver carts full of lemons and tomatoes
milk in plastic jugs with red and yellow bands
(you take whole in tea, but skim with cereal)

A cathedral stood where we slept
stained glass headboard
the dust hung above
a spire where you draped your coat

Michael Slepian Studies Secrets – Jen Schneider (she/her)

Michael Slepian studies secrets. All thirty-eight varieties. I'm not the
only one intrigued. His work, the focus of many honors. A rising star
award recipient. His book, a regular top seller. Curiosity surmised.
Michael Slepian studies secrets. Of which there are many. I read on.
I learn that the average human holds thirteen secrets at any given
time, and I wonder. About weight and waiting. For relief. I don't
believe it's the quantity that intrigues me most. It's more than a fear
of zero-sum games. More than an uneasiness around baker's
dozens and the number thirteen. It's the weight of the silence. How
heavy that must be. Bad for the shoulders. A strain on lower back
muscles. The weight of extramarital affairs. The forbidden foods
(red meat / yellow cake) snuck after carefully designed plant-based
lunches. The breaches of privacy. The broken vows. The slips of
tongue. Red No. 2 dye and theories of aliens not far flung. Michael
Slepian studies secrets. How heavy that must be. The forbidden
romances. The hotel happenstances. The overdrafts. The
underwear. I sit on the medical exam table (buttocks bare) and
dictate with no emotion. My face a sheet of poker blanks. All cards
concealed. The doctor scribbles. With nary a care for the obvious
thirteen. Michael Slepian studies secrets. Breaches and leeches.
Crushes and near-revelatory brushes. Social disappointments.
Missed mental health appointments. My back broken. Prescriptions
often overused. A useless proposition for a habitual, often innocent
proclamation. The scholar suggests release. Muscles tense than
tango with forehead creases. Shame a rhyming word for elementary
school games. Lost babies rhyme with moss and maybes. Grassy
meadows beatings chime (both in and out of tune) with broken
window cheatings. The weight of secrets carried since childhood
both a blessing and a shame. Musical chairs and Candyland more
predictable than unachieved fame. An equal likelihood of outcomes

and chance. Shoe boxes stuffed in closets. Purchases and promises wrapped in wrinkled tissue paper. Layers of lemonade yellow and cotton candy pink. Tags still attached. Credit cards shorted. Department store air both artificial and heavily perfumed. Clive Christian No.1. Chanel No. 5. Hermes 24 Faubourg. Liquid joy. Conspiratorial toys. Michael Slepian studies secrets. Each of us carry, on average, thirteen. I wonder about the number—neither divine nor refined. I've never been superstitious, but I can't deny the hesitation I feel each time I think of confidants. Of children. Of companions. And wonder about the weight of their secrets. Dung, drugs, and purchases hidden under rugs (shag) and shrugs. Hobbies and political lobbies. Addictions and prescriptions. Would it tip a scale or turn a tide. What would each of us think if we revealed. Abortion already high on the list, Slepian reveals. Voice calm. Emotions metered. It's research all the same. I wonder about the birds at the window. Sometimes red. Sometimes blue. A rotating carousel of vibrant hues. Does the weight of the world's secrets bear down on their feathers, too? Are birds and bees a purely human quality? And the gal at the hospital (the one with no thirteenth floor) in candy stripes. She accepts the flowers—roses and lilacs / poinsettias and pansies. Waters both bouquets. Dusts faux wood. Repositions floral confections. *Aren't they nice*, she might say. Cards tucked. Lips sealed. It's sponge bath day. Water seeps. All beings porous. We struggle. Grab then gaggle. Quick dry towels. Syllables concealed behind overgrown jowls. Michael Slepian studies secrets. How heavy that must be. Of extraterrestrial beings. Elevator secrets. Rendezvous. Skipped floors. Skipped periods. Commas and extended moments of pause. Days of misfortune. Tales both Canterbury and contrite. In the small pockets of air where dust hasn't yet settled, I wonder about the weight of the secrets. Those we freeze. Those we boil. All kettles on. Our backs (burners never spared) shoulders to the steam. I wonder how the record players and research trackers have persisted since quarantine. (Raging) secrets, (rare) solitude, and (rock) candy stripes. Money (bills and banks) and music (ballads and blues). Finances (credit checks) and freelancers (cross-checked). Bedrooms (birds and bees) and bites (bee stings and Tastykakes quietly consumed). Sex (soiled) and dirty socks (toiled). Shoplifters (elusive) and story seekers (compulsive). Secrets in plain sight. Michael Slepian studies secrets. All thirty-eight varieties. Each of us harboring an average of thirteen. How heavy that must be.

Cosmos Meets Chaos on the Gravel Path, Just Off the Interstate (& its Shadow) – Jen Schneider (she/her)

i walk on (onto) the gravel path, the one just off the interstate, & just beyond the double-sided sign. the rusted metal reads (screams in large block font, once red, now shaded pink blush) WELCOME. NO TRESPASSING appears (perhaps peers) on the other of the rectangular post. no one pays much attention to the park rules. all signs (trash cans, pails lined of plastic, parking lots, spots lined of diesel) signal it's time to either come or go. comers pick their own path. traced & tracked.

a biker approaches. on an off roader. oversized rubber wheels secured to an undersized metal frame. posture straight. thighs pulse as they peddle. chest clothed of tightly fitted lycra. a jersey—Campbell's soup. its subtext reads "full of beans". i check my watch. confirm both time & place. it's neither late march nor a setting for merch. the local Campbell's factory, on the other side of the river, shuttered years ago.

the biker appears ageless. twenty. times two. i lose count. a white crane rests on a nearby rock. baby ducks waddle behind a mother goose. the biker cruises as if he has answers to questions i never knew to ask. he carries the weight of the forest on his back & peddles toward the crossing. where the gravel cracks. where north meets south. & all signs change.

he wears thick goggles with wide rims. secured of elastic straps. trappings of time & stone. an unexpected gust of wind flusters nearby limbs. amidst weariness of many stages, his legs continue to cycle. muscles neither entrapped nor contrived. confidence bred of beans & proteins.

i have a sudden craving for a bowl of soup. & long to climb the flight of steps—gates to the heavens—at the public pool, down the road, on the other side of the interstate. the one with the sign that makes all intentions clear. CLOSED. & dive. feet first. arms wide. like the crane. into a bowl of beans. & strip metal cans of labels. & ride like the man (perhaps a/the god) on the two wheeler. & carry answers on backs. amidst myths & legends. of time. place. & beans.

a small toad burps. hyacinths wave. lilac scented brush kiss shoulders. i
sneeze. of truth. & telling myths. a/the god recedes into the near &
present future. distance dances the waltz. the toad burps. again.
i wonder where he's headed. his head high. of sky & flora. all limbs
locked. my shadow shivers. the trail nothing more than the unknown. a
collection of gravel & grain. where idle ideas irk the isolated. &
hammers meet nails. wild iris bouquets. layers of lilies. no trespassing
signs stretched across trunks.

i envy his freedom. to be. to go. to pedal. my own two wheels locked in
a shadow with no key. always on clocks. i walk into my own shadow.
legs mimic limits. winds blow. limbs grow. days lengthen even as suns
set.

i think of tales
of the jersey devil
& wonder
if it has a map
            or a tail

never good at geography
always crossing lines
of state, stature, & circumstance

        despite no trespassing signs

a four-leaf clover
whistles
        then screams
in/against/of
        winds with no echo

i walk into my shadow.
as rotations of limits linger.
all compasses spiral.

the gravel darker. the sun less bright
& i wonder if the jersey is a statement
on beans and beef. Americans
doing their best to harm the Amazon
Amazon doing its best to harm America

so much i wish to know.

what happens
when/if what
i fear most of death
is meeting the living

whether devils
dressed in denim
& lace are daring or dangerous

what if not only towers but skies
fall with no warning

twenty-twenty vision
out of reach
goggles muddied
the biker is gone
with neither testimony,
stain, nor trace

his Campbell's jersey
          —full of beans

lies on a bench

          to the right

his shadow vanishes

to the left

my eyes dart,

      right

left

         up

          down

all laces tied. a frog burps

a/the god at play

& haiku fall
like drops of rain

       a large white crane
       swoops then scoops
       an 8-ounce bag of *Lays*

       an empty metal
       bench buckles
       under the weight of shadows

       a gray cigarette butt
       lays at the base
       of a half rainbow

i gather the butt,

      sit on the bench,

& cradle

      the Campbell's
      beans
      jersey

That's How He Was Made
/ A Refection (of Questionable Testimony
& Unquestionable Melody) on Jerry Lee Lewis – Jen Schneider
(she/her)

Great balls of fire erupted. In tune. In time. On stages. On radio airwaves. Across keys. Across zip codes. Up and down highway corridors. Up and down regional parlor halls. Crowds would cheer. Hands held high. Bodies clothed in trends of decades. Denim and leather. Fringe and lace. Grease and grime. Hips swayed. Movements in (and across) time. Marriage and mayhem. Melodies and majors. That's how he was made. Jerry Lee Lewis electrified. He'd belt tunes with a swagger. Cut notes with a dagger. Unify crowds. Deepen divides. Hit the high notes—on loud. Heat the stage—on replay. Inspired flames. Never tame. That's how he was made. Jerry Lee Lewis electrified. Performance in his DNA. He wouldn't have it any other way. Genres as layered as labels. Labels on perpetual (re)call. Age a number. Performance cues his daily muse. An originator. A rock. A roll. A roller. A preacher's dream. Best and worst combined. All hands (and feet) on piano keys. All keys divine. Self-taught. Self-made. A byproduct of the Grand Ole Opry and the Louisiana Hayride. That's how he was made. Incomparable. Unfollowable. Unflappable. Great balls of fire. Jerry Lee Lewis. A master of time and place. A father. A player. A singer. An entertainer. A preacher. A uniter. A divider. An electrifiable performer. Jerry Lee Lewis magnetized. Wheels spinning. Lyrics streaming. From dawn to dusk. From youth to lust. For more. Time. To perform. To create. To reimagine. To reincarnate. The divine. A first. A voice that would last. And withstand the ultimate tests. An inductee. Rock and Roll Hall of Famer. A beat inescapable. A controversial fella. Undeniable. Across billboards. Across coasts. A self-taught possessor of a litany of mosts. A mover. A shaker. A whole lot of maker. Great balls of fire. That's how he was made. Jerry Lee Lewis electrified. His flame still strong. His mark deeply ingrained. We bid not farewell but a thank you. Of sorts. Twisted and entwined with acknowledgment of the turbulence. Of gospel. Of rockabilly. Of rocky times. The terror. The less than refine. We bow. We respect. We extend grace. For the music. For the memories. For the moments turned minutes turned melodies. Until "Another Place, Another Time". Jerry Lee Lewis. Your music. Your swagger. Your hits. Your daggers. Melodies continue to wind through time. Over forty albums. Seven decades and counting. Performance purer than personhood. In fear of the devil. In servitude for forgiveness. Of hardcore hits and visions that never looked tried. Of retries and rises. Of hard times (beats and beatings) and hobbies (fountain pens). Of classics and comebacks. Of trials and rewinds. It's been a while. Of broken will. Of beats and bleats. Of windpipes and pin-tucked stripes. *What a thrill.* That's how he was made. Jerry Lee Lewis electrified.

inducted in 1986 (divided by 40 albums) (less seven-plus decades) / reasons to (de)cry - great balls of fire

Initial inductees offer a guarantee. Tunes and tombs of flamboyant fire.

1. A roll of hips. A gamble on (d)ice. Piano keys both innovate and stabilize.

2. Fingers and toes equally appropriate music makers.

3. As much a taker as a shaker. A teacher and a self-taught improviser.

4. Talents often refine with age. A prime stake. An inductee of incomparable make.

5. No stranger to pain or heartbreak (rules often broken). Comebacks less token than betwixt. Of controversy both real and contrived. An indelible (perpetual) remix.

6. A member of both the Country and Rock and Roll Halls of Fame. Tapes and escapes.

7. Admired by Presley and Cash. Fans willing to pay for a spot in a standing-room mash.

8. Not all movers and shakers are makers. Not all makers are movers or shakers.

9. A rare combination of country, rock, and roll. Of rockabilly. In need of accountability.

10. A maker of *Olde Tyme Country Music* and *Boogie Woogie Country Man*.

11. A billboard climber. Knees never primer. Eager to cut records and to conquer clubs.

12. A blend of high and low notes. Of farm mortgages and homemade fan thrillers.

13. A defiant crowd-pleaser. Highly (s)killed. A master of leaving audiences "*Breathless*".

14. A crafter of chorus. A curator of controversies. A history both complex and layered.

15. A self-made student. A self-taught teacher. A master of the quintessentially (in)formal.

16. Lewis's lyrics linger in layers. His musical notes self-made (less crowd control).

17. A crown jewel running on infinite fuel. Subject to infinite questions.

18. A *"Whole lotta shakin…"* audience pleaser. An electric teaser.

19. Powerful notes. Piano playing totes. Always the last. Always ending on a high note.

—What a thrill. That's how he was made.

Jerry Lee Lewis electrified.

Murmur in Chronic Town – Lawrence Miles (he/him)

It ended violently
The great beast tumbling down
A sickening thud that was not replayed

The ratings for the spectacle
Would never be repeated
But it was something not picked up by any camera
Which would linger in the memory

"Well it's over, the airplanes got him" someone said
"No" was the response
"It wasn't the airplanes
It was beauty killed the beast"

An intense murmur of confusion
Echoed through the masses
Trying to decipher what they heard

There were soon rumors of a woman
That the creature had loved
But she was never identified

Because it happened so close to Thanksgiving
It was the subject around dinner tables
For years to come
Some still trying to understand
How beauty had slain the beast
While others thought the whole thing
A hoax perpetrated on the people

"No such thing as monsters" they would say
Digging into Brussel sprouts
Even when rumors of another creature
Sighted off the coast of Japan
Began to create their own murmurs.

The Empty Chair – Linda Doran (she/her)

At our dinner table there is an empty chair,
A void in our home for the one who can't be there.
We remember other years, the memories remain,
But Christmas without them is never quite the same.
There are no presents wrapped for them underneath the tree.
An empty space now exists where their gift should be.
All the little traditions that were built through the years,
We try to carry with us as we fight back secret tears.
We try to cook their recipes the way they used to do,
But nothing tastes the same with a heart broken in two.
So we buy ornaments of angels and hang them on the tree.
Every robin makes us wonder if it's them we really see.
We lay wreathes on their graves and set candles alight.
We search for shooting stars in the sky late at night.
All these little rituals are the things that get us through,
Reminders that our loved ones are part of everything we do.
Nobody is certain of what the future holds,
Whose chair might next be empty as the year unfolds.
So cherish your loved ones, let the small things go.
Eat the cake, drink the wine, build angels in the snow.
Time is the greatest gift and the least expensive too,
Gift it wholeheartedly and receive it back to you.

Untitled Tankas – Katherine E. Winnick (she/her)

shimmering moon
swans gliding through darkness
reflections abound
ducklings rest beneath trees
whilst a lotus blooms

A

Falling Leaf

Leaves its tree

With branches bending

Slowly with plums dropping

Speeding past in the fast lane

Squirrels scouring at its roots

Feathers twirling in the wind

Rolling around on the grass

A cat curls in delight

The scent of blossom

In the air

Earth

*

made to perfection
origami paper crane
hues of black and green
depicting my forest walk
and the cawing crow

Accidental School – Fabrice Poussin (he/him)

Any place will do, to hide and find
an old machine-gun, a little rusty
and the meds with an expired date.

Good for nothing now, can't kill
can't save a life either, but
perhaps child's play will do.

Cartridges of pills and powder
crumbling in a singular shine
mix neatly with the ground
on the makeshift shrine.

Alone behind the secret cages
attentive, the little surgeon
he plays with life unaware.

The scent intrigues, the flame arises
unexpected without a spark, fumes
like mustard gas so precarious.

No story to tell friends next day
of the domain of another truth
the adventure on the edge of life
is too grand to be believed.

Soon time for dinner and bed
leaving behind the scientist's dream
shorts hanging again near the slumber
memories already distant of the experiment
he closes his eyes on visions of colors
magical sights he creates night and day
little alchemist the world is his
so long as tomorrow again he lives.

Holiday – Fabrice Poussin (he/him)

The furious siren tore through the air
while multicolored lights shone all around
in a quiet neighborhood of exclusive souls.

Onlookers slowed to a crawl as they questioned
with a gaze their jolly passengers
who for a moment stilled their jitters.

Trunks overflowing with boxes wrapped
in holiday colors of greens, golds, and reds
soon come to busy their mind again.

While not far, surgeons and nurses rush
to welcome yet another casualty of our days
wrapped in a blanket of fevers, fears, and endings.

Those may be the merry days of the year
yet how many suffer such despair
as their neighbors revel in carols.

How many will slip into so much uncertainty
see their beloved sisters perish in a sea of horrors
come home to the silence of utter abandon?

This is the mood of our lives
filled with smiles, laughter, and agony
so quick to overtake even the sweetest of times.

With a Wave – Fabrice Poussin (he/him)

From a distance
he hopes
witness to a common spectacle
he seeks to capture the wave.

At the closing of the days
a ritual ceremony
space makes way for her departure
a void remains in the darkness.

A mere sign written upon the air
warm with the glow of infinite comets
leaves a trace to be cherished
slowly to spread through eternity.

Then nothing
the apparition vanishes once again
her footsteps echoing into the abyss
the farewell a treasure to him who remains.

Grin and Childbear It – Allison Fradkin (she/her)

Once upon a time,
the platitude was:
Beggars can't be choosers.
Today we're Wade-ing into the attitude:
Eggers can't be choosers.
Why not let her be?
Why take the letter B,
the A for autonomy,
the C for choice?
It's bad enough that you
deemphasize and
dehumanize her.
Must you
de-alphabetize her as well?
But then, the ball is no longer
in her court
It's being bounced on
fertile ground
and hapless hips.
Because the Supremes' baby love
has given her the shaft
and the bundle of joy
its reception may result in.
I can just hear the majority humming
your infantilizing victory song
as you over-the-moonwalk on air:
Breed it, just breed it.
Well, she doesn't have to be
Janet Jackson
to take control,
so you can beat it
like Michael would roll.
It's really that simple.

Because when you take the pro
out of reproductive
you get reductive.
So you may not want to
rejoice yet.
Because she's going to
re-choice yet
again.
Her fight's not over.
It's ovaried.
Dissatisfied with your
vote-by-*male* system,
she's not only planning to
rock the boat.
She's planning to
Roe it.
As a matter of fact,
she's giving birth
to the totally
fallopian
tubular
concept
that yes, she can
uterise up
and take you down.
You must
support that babe
up in arms.
After all, you believe that
life begins
at conception,
right?

I Love Lezzie – Allison Fradkin (she/her)

It all started during a vacation from marriage.
Not mine—Lucy Ricardo's.
Naturally, Ethel takes a hiatus
from her husband too,
and Lucy moves in with
—though not in on—
her gal pal.
But all hope is not lost,
least of all when Lucy lets loose
with this loaded remark: *I hope you boys*
are going to have as gay an evening
as we are.
(You know, they really were pioneer women, those two,
what with all the accidental advocating they did
for marriage equality.)

Okay, so maybe that remark really wasn't so gay,
given the time period in which it was uttered,
but I chose to take it the right way:
as permission to
define,
refine,
and redefine
my sexuality.
I could do more than identify
as a member
of the LGBT community.

I could ident-defy:
as
Liberated,
Grateful,
Bodacious,
and Tenacious.

Seeing this revelation
as cause for celebration,
I went singin' in the rainbow
that I prefer dolls to guys.
Mama said there'll be gays like this:
those who embrace their sexuality straight away,
not only because they've figured out
that the bloom is off the heteros;
but also because,
in the words of midcentury chanteuse Dinah Washington,
What a diff'rence a gay makes
or, you know, something a little more fifties-friendly
like:
I love lezzie and she loves me
Queer as happy as two can be…

Challah If You Queer Me – Allison Fradkin (she/her)

Everything I need to know about being Jewish I learned from
The Nanny:

Every meshugeneh needs a mensch
Don't schlep—get married already!
If you're over thirty and single
you might be—
—it's likely—
you're gay
(Oy vey!)
There'll be kvetching and kibitzing
You'll become a Jewcy bit of gossip
People will say pish, you're just *farmisht*
Your mishpochah will plotz
Start packing for your guilt trip
(Guilt: Just Jew it)

But what if you can't forget
about that little matzo ball of fire
you met at the synagogue
The one with charm and chutzpah
who makes your eyes light up like a menorah
your head spin like a dreidel
and your heart chant *Hava Nagila*
every time you look at her

For Hashem's sake
—and your own—
don't let some schmendricks
rain on your pride parade
or make you feel like schmutz on a schmatte
or pressure you to take their verkakte-mamie advice:
At least date a non-goy boy before you make it official!

Instead, get them to kiss your keppie like everything's kosher,
because wonder of wonder,
queer-acle of queer-acles,
it is

So trade that guilt for (chocolate) gelt
break out the bubbly grape juice
and propose a toast:
to life
to love
to loving your life
and the *meydl* with the *sheyn ponem* in it
Your chosen person
Your finest Frantasy

Just do it with justifiable Jewbilance

rainy days – Val Langford (she/they)
CW: Sexual assault, self harm

Even when the clouds stop raining,
the trees do not;
the storm ends and
the remnants shall remain.

Five years later, my body still trembles
when hands are laid upon it,
even if they are of a platonic intention.
Thunderous heart warning,
cloudy eyes in the distance.

Flashbacks are not deja vu, they are
flashbacks; remnants remaining of
lightning bolts,
the splintered, fallen trees,
the charred land and burnt fields;
memories so far buried, we've forgotten
where the headstones lie.

I feel hands on my thighs; not yours,
and suddenly I am afraid.
I am supposed to be in your presence,
but his remains.
My hands carve out his fingerprints
as if to remind me they aren't there
anymore

Present moment calls me with
reddened drops puddling in my hand,
the culprit clouded, already gone, but the
remnants of the rain remain.

she said – Sophie Morelli (she/her)

she said she's been stewing in this for years. that she crawled right up out of the puddle in my driveway because someone told her it was the hudson. she says i'll never need to count your ribs again because she snapped clean off of one of them and she holds your marrow in her teeth. she says she'll make me better. she lets me talk about your good parts. she picks your fingernails from the skin of my back. she says it's okay to borrow things. she says learning my blood is learning bravery, that hiding from bruises is useless, that bloody girls go to prom with a bucket. she says all bones are good bones. she says worry through all of it, but don't show it. she says whatever is in my guts wants out, that she speaks the same language as my lungs. she says sometimes Mother is evil, sometimes she is a ghost, sometimes she grows on the grapevine. she says sometimes my days will be enamel parades, but sometimes, my footsteps will be the smallest. she says I am the syrup in the morning, the sunlight baking the coffee table. she says she's memorized my days and that I have all of them left.

A Resumé – Sophie Morelli (she/her)

One thing about me is that I can't eat cherry pie. I used to eat cherries up, and then I got the stomach bug and actually this feels a little like that. Another thing is I talk in my sleep. Only when you're listening. I am in love more often than I am not. I pray by singing I Think We're Alone Now into the end of my Swiffer. I got a roll of quarters so big we could get to Massachusetts. If you bring a map. I feel good in a way I'm skeptical of. I'll pretend all your card tricks work when they don't; I am amazed by magic even when it's fake. My momma taught me about spicy food and that I Do Not Like It. My momma taught me to write what you know, which is why all my poems are love poems. She taught me about red, and the blues, and how everything is one of those two. But what about you? Are you okay? Are you sure you're okay? Are you sure about anything? Would you teach me to play cards again? I used to know how when my dad was around, but now all I know is five-card. I think I am good at this. I am out of left field, which I hear is your favorite seat. I have a firework mouth because I'm full of personality. A great contender. An A-plus candidate. How can I hear you say no over all this noise?

What do you do with your grief? – Sophie Morelli (she/her)

My grief gives everyone kid gloves.
Makes everyone put on a face like
they don't want to say I have broccoli in my teeth.
My grief gives me a thousand conversations that are
Botox-tight in the name of saving face.

How do I get someone to tell me something with
some pins and needles? Why has nobody asked
me if the next sharp thing I touch will shatter me?
People build walls and walls until you look up and
realize there are no windows.

Look at you with your grief—you thought it
peeked out like a pocket square from your
collar when everyone else has seen it for its
suitcase. You drag your grief around on a leash.
Like a creature in a zoo. People stay behind the
glass, like as long as someone else is
feeding that thing they will pay a bit to take a look,
enter your grief for a moment.

When my grief is old enough to enter first grade,
why does no one ask why it feels like a hot fresh wound?
Why the scar is not pink yet?
What do you do with this stain you cannot get out of yourself?

What's the word for a thing that you cannot let go of;

for a thing that will not let go of you?

How do I convince everyone that my fragile is gone

when it seeps out of me like jam from a pie crust

Like rain through that busted roof

Like sun through a magnifying glass

Like sun through a magnifying glass?

If Therapy was Free – Anna Emilia (she/her)

If therapy was free
The World would be at peace
No more talking heads
Political machines
Striving to keep us divided
Our differences highlighted
Heal from the trauma that plagues us
With useless, printed money
Paying us for our souls
Paying us to withhold
Mainstream bribes
Trendy blackmail
To forget who we are
Convenient amnesia
If therapy was free
We could just express
But, unfortunately, our first couch was insurance
Some money is dirty
Constantly exchanged
       Through different hands, same energies

Fatal Firework – Stuti (she/her)

Tongues of tangerine stoke *slow* burn
          as they lick her heels in anticipatory air
Static pops and crackles crawl up her throat
          purveying plumes of sulfurous breaths

She flickers ablaze towards the milky moon
          shattering to s-h-r-a-p-n-e-l-s and shards
                    splitting into splinters and burning showers

In a kaleidoscope of freckled luminescence
          She disintegrates as stars on fire
They carouse in the canopy of her cremation
          while heaven grieves in tears of pulverized debris

She—an evanescent extravaganza
          is baptized to end by a fatal spark;
Thus transcending from
          dazzling spotlights to lingering dark

While they wonder,
          could there be a more alluring demise?

* First Published in Sky Island Journal

Marl Grey Jumper – Stuti (she/her)

…And I want to dress every day in this boyfriend-style, marl grey and white striped jumper.

i.

Your eyes widen as you walk in my direction/ I am taken by that/ unprepared to stun you in something so casual/ Your expression followed by intimately whispered affection gives me a tingle deep in my belly/ the 'happy accident' kind of tingle/ the small sprinkles of euphoria are big winners kind of tingle/

Like sitting on the desk of a swanky young office/ in an unpretentious slouchy jumper/ jeans/ and white trainers/ legs swinging mid-air/ enjoying the misplaced quietness of that environment/ I take a small sip/ into the silken foam of a warm cappuccino/

ii

In a few minutes/ this silence will crescendo to/ a business *hustle-bustle*/ the incessant ringing of multiple telephones/ voices talking in loud pitch/ over other voices/ the smell of cartridges printing/ *(wet ink on paper)*/ doors swinging into //repeating// open & close motions/ the receptionist's dull voice clinically receiving calls on the board line/ *(in practiced politeness)*/ more coffee/ pouring from a dispensing machine into **countless** mugs/

Cold conditioned air/ coated with the smell of fresh paint/ there is always the smell of fresh paint/ in a paint manufacturing office/ like there is the smell of freshly baked bread at a bakery/ (*I wonder if bakers are as tired of the smell of baking bread as I am of the smell of fresh paint)/*

iii

more sounds/ delivery boxes dropping with heavy thuds/ (on carpeted floors)/ feet shuffling/ more telephone ringing/ more voices/

It is no wonder then/ that this current silence is a small sprinkle of euphoria/ even sweeter than the 6 am silence of waking up in a house/ where everyone/ *(the dachshund and the birds on the terrace included)/* is still sleeping/

Like the sweetness of this moment/ when you spot the jumper hugging my frame/ better than the collective sweetness of all those moments/ when I meticulously put myself together for you/

*First Published in *Moss Puppy Magazine*

Monarch March – Daniel Moreschi (he/him)

A streak of weightless specks seem guided by beguiling light
To round a trackless pathway, where familiar hills invite
Them to descend on sweeping boughs. They drape the dews and fuse
With branches, forming tapestries of golden-orange hues.

Once nascent rays of dawn survey these dormant swathes, it brings
A timely warmth that wakes an inner wish in them that sings
A skyward symphony. They flit in sync to swiftly form
The frenzied sways and whirling clusters of a twinkling swarm.

They criss-cross past the groves and glades, to where a net of streams
Amalgamates their bursts with binds along invisible seams:
A funnelled climb towards the clouds, until horizons wear
Their gushing flushes as they dive and jive through aisles of air.

They flow in growing droves and reach beyond an ocean's span
To render an aurora pose above Michoacán
And patter on the firs to prove a cycle rebegun:
The rise and fall of monarchs who forever chase the sun.

the evanescent goodbye – Nazmi Shaikh (she/her)

tonight, I must let you go
your eyes catch mine as a stranger's gaze
bestrewn with ambiguity and unrevealed affair
holding her hand tighter so you wouldn't give it away
I had to leave—buy the ticket from the nearest station
mount the first train I see, for I do not wish to lag behind
only to land somewhere I do not recognize
the land's water chokes me—almost as if it did not want me there
must I leave yet again?
wandering west—searching for a less cruel place
I will not become a wife   simply a sightseer
I am not dubious—it's simply that:
to have all is to lose some
some of you, some of me
some of us

Lunchbox – Deron Eckert (he/him)

What little is left of my childhood
fits into a lunchbox with room
left for the thermos that still smells
like your vegetable soup even
though it is wiped clean and empty.

Fox scout badges and worthless cards
rest below letters from girls who
speak of forever, not knowing
what little is left.

They could not imagine they would
be forgotten any more than I
thought I would ever forget them.
I can't even picture them, but
I still smell your soup and cherish
what little is left.

October Darling. – Fritz Dries (he/him)

when autumn begins to unlace her
boots after a long day of work,

when the lazy maple stoops too far
to collect her shedding mane,
drunk and drained with cherry cheeks
and a grin caught in gold,

when winter waits outside the door
eager to be let in,
my lover lives there.

my lover with her hair on fire
and eyes like morning Arctic pools.
she is all the beauty of a shifting season.

Medusa in the way she holds me
still,
so still.
to move would be to miss her.

Seasonal Labour. – Fritz Dries (he/him)

The men in this family talk on eggshells.
Careful words from a dead bird. Grandma grew up killing chickens,
and you can't even call the doctor. Come on.
Want to be a man in this family?
You look like him, now act like it. Take something and drown it.
Smile.
Talk about it when you're dead. Or someone else will, what does it
matter?
The men in this family hurt themselves. Or get hurt and stay that
way.
And really, what's the difference?
Help is an uncomfortable jacket. Something Dad taught you.
Half a finger gone, let's finish our coffee first.
Don't make the cut, just control how long it hurts. How bad it heals.
Scar up, son. The men in this family need character.
Get back to work, we need something to be proud of.

War Is for Dogs [And Other Human Myths]. – Fritz Dries (he/him)

This war is going to be different. Everyone is saying so.
All the stomachs are turning. All the tongues are wagging.
This is going to be a big one, boys.
We're going to need every warm body. No fellow left behind.

This war, we recruit the dogs.

Line 'em up. Shave 'em down.
Get on with it,
these bullets need loving homes.

"Oh, won't you *please* come on down,
you're *such* a good boy, yes you *are!*
That's it. Ease into the line,
and remember to lie down when we tell you."

No Exit Wound. – Fritz Dries (he/him)

Here I am drawing on the exit wound
with a red pen.
You can call this healing
because it looks like healing,
but the bullet is still here,
it never left my skin.
Here, let me pretend the problem is
out of my system.
Let me pretend this will heal.
I don't want to make you hurt me
again.

Look, I'm getting better,
so you can wash up now,
and
forget I said anything.

Confab – Marisa Silva-Dunbar (she/her)

I.

This was all I asked for: a simple meeting to unravel/ the stories told
to us. You denied it so quickly, but it showed me your true face.//
You claim to be a healer, swear that your hands and voice can
soothe—/ bring a spiritual mentor to tears as she curls into a child's
pose./ I went to you asking for a remedy for all the lies/ you laughed
and fed me more slick, biled misinformation, unaware/ that I was
present when you embodied desperation/ another woman begging
to be loved, not interested in sharing truths.

II.

I used to imagine us: Late fall—when the streets are crunchy with
cottonwood leaves/ It's mid-morning and the sun can't help but
shine/ through the big windows of this crowded cafe./ Sit next to
me on this soft velvet couch./ people mistake us for friends—and in
this moment, I don't mind./ I sip regally from a tea cup/while you
try to warm your hands on a to-go cup of white mocha./ My red
lipstick leaves a perfect print on the rim of cup; my winged liner/ is
so sharp it could cut you if you tried to remove a lash to make a
wish on.

III.

In the daydream tell you: "Through your multiple facades I see the
jewel of you that you hide/—that you don't even know exists/
always trying to find the right girl to be so that someone could love
you just a little more./ I now know your hashtags are wishes/ how
you want to be seen/ and loved/ what you want your life to grow
into.// You cannot thrive, when home is a battleground and the
prize is affection./"

IV.

A confession: I wonder if that gem exists or if the potential I saw
was always a mirage?

V.

Here is a theory full of mixed metaphors:/ We are mirrors for one
another—and there are days/ when we can write "you are
beautiful" in Magenta Minx/ lipstick, and others when we cringe at
each blemish,/ turn away from each scar—a reminder of frantic
mistakes; an urgent cry for validation in pushup bras and red high
heels.// We are two South Pole magnets who will never be able to
connect peacefully/ neither of us longs to turn into a true North/
whatever that may mean./ I realize this only matters to me.

I never put your numbers in my phone – Marisa Silva-Dunbar
(she/her)

During a soul exchange five years ago,
I imagined I pulled out a gold chain inlaid
with rubies and diamonds from your throat.
The version of you that I loved died ten years
before; I no longer needed to be tethered

to that illusion. Did you want this goodbye
to be devastating? I hadn't realized I had packed
up mental and emotional baggage months before.
Whatever power you thought you had over me,
dissipated—evaporated over the years.

We will each go back to lives that fulfill us,
find new and old friends for company at our dinner
tables. Although mine won't only think about themselves
when they come to feast, or celebrate me on my birthday—
something you never could be bothered showing up for.

The desperation of cuffing season – Marisa Silva-Dunbar (she/her)

Over coffee she confides: *it's better to be with someone
you didn't want to kiss in early spring to late summer,
than it is to be alone come autumn.* She sighs that occasionally
her stomach still churns, still aches when his lips touch
hers because she can't pretend he's *the one*.
She wants to turn away when he leans in for a kiss.

Sometimes she panics when he mentions
purchasing one of the new flats downtown near
the river. He's told her what kind of cabinets he wants
in the kitchen, that pendant lighting will suit
their lifestyle best. He buys her trinkets and charms
to decorate her ankles and neck; she daydreams

about other men sucking champagne from her navel
and breasts. She tries to rewrite history about
how they met; she tells her friends and family
she was the prey and he was the skillful nimrod—
the seducer, he made it so easy to bend to his will.
She doesn't tell them about how he paid for her time,

or how often she passed him over—stood him up;
how she'd whine *he's so boring!!!!* to an anonymous
internet audience, whenever he'd suggest a film
or dinner at the lake. But she smiles eagerly at me,
says it's better to tell the tale of a soft, insipid romance
—how just for a moment she's dazzled into believing
her own sugary little lies. This too is loneliness.

Possibilities – Marisa Silva-Dunbar (she/her)

At twenty, I wanted to ask you to follow me across the ocean; I
imagined we would have been like Frida and Diego, or Ted and
Sylvia—holed up in a flat, colors spilling over. Our living room—a
jungle of hothouse flowers, peach blossoms and jasmine bursting
out of their jars, sweating into our skin.

We'd spend afternoons in the pub people watching, note taking;
you'd write about your newest muse, the girl who stole sugar
from the coffeehouse around the corner. I'd send tattered
postcards home—mementos from our weekend trips to various
villages

and the vineyards. We'd go out to museums and nightclubs,
where your eyes darted away from me, looking for other potential
lovers. We'd decorate our apartment with cherry wood furniture
and silk tapestries. Our place would be cluttered with unfinished
masterpieces,

your Dunhills and my manuscripts would litter our coffee table.
There'd be highball glasses with lipstick stains leftover from the
night you brought the philosophy student home, while I was visiting
a friend in London. For others this would be the beginning of the
end—

we'd feast on the drama, ignite insecurities and desires; we'd
compete over who could hurt the other most when flirting with fit
bartenders, and messy women we met on the dance floor. We'd nip
at each other's flesh, leave nail marks for others to find—let this
toxic love consume us.

But I was silent, so you never came. That fall I went out to bars,
pining over arrogant and ridiculous men, while you succumbed to
the lure of a mouthy little bitch. She'd strut around your bedroom in
stilettos and a black fedora and you'd release an orgasmic sigh over
a dirty martini and cigarette.

Something new – Marisa Silva-Dunbar (she/her)

Tuesday and the city seems like it was captured
on pocket instamatic film—the hazy blue sky
held up by the rugged, dusty brown of the Sandias;
the moon rises in her opaque glory.

I head east as a new love reads poetry to me. She created
a soundtrack with the whiny tinkle of a piano,
and dappled interplanetary bells and beeps.
Her voice feels like she is waiting for me cliff side,

or in an orange orchard in the afternoon.
It has been months since I felt new poetry curl
my fingertips, point my toes. There is no cracking
of the heart like an egg. No longing or rage stored

My fingernails – Jillian Calahan (she/her/they)

My fingernails
never seem to be
clean underneath.
No matter how many times
I wash my hands,
a little dirt always remains.
And I'm reminded of
the scratches on my skin.
The tiny scabs dotting
my arms and legs where
I dug just a little too deep.
My fingernails never seem
to be clean underneath.
Maybe because I'm always
trying to claw my way out
of this skin.

Listen For The Children's Laughter – Jillian Calahan (she/her/they)
For the children of Uvalde, Texas

Listen for the children's laughter,
is there anything so sweet?
With the buzz of summer giggles
they wiggle wildly in their seats.

Eager to run through lemon sunshine
and search for animals in disguise
in puffy cotton candy clouds
among the blue raspberry skies.

The time has come for school to end
just a few more days to go.
Excited to hear of their summer plans
but now we'll never know

The sirens scream out once again
as we hear the breaking news.
Tell me when did a child's classroom
become their final tomb?

We listen for the children's laughter,
but sweetness has no sound
when we face the task of burying
nineteen children in the ground.

And they sugar coat their speeches,
send us useless thoughts and prayers,
while they stand up for the NRA,
but address us sitting from their chairs.

Now our ears are filled with bitter talk
for whom to blame this violence.
We listen for our children's laughter
but now all we hear is silence.

Upkeep – Keon Wong (he/him)

Say to me
The same things
You have said to
Every other person;
Anything else
Is indigestion.

Woodpecker, woodpecker—a body
Of rot knocking on doors of stale earth.
I've eaten more worms than you
Even when I only feast in dreams.
Tighten that red-banded neck, that
Dangerously bulbous eye—you might as well
Be an automaton; you remind me
Of when men only need a house and a house only.

Let your voice curdle
In the bending heat, let the wind
Jostle it like honey. Feel the lump in your throat
Growing like a seed. I can't bear it
Anymore—the sun through the window is too bright
Even when the day has long ended.
When did the bees last sleep?
When was the last time you had heard
The procession of the lullabies?

Obligatory – Keon Wong (he/him)

Nothing can stop the rolling bells,
The low hum before midnight,
The cicadas, dreaming of bugles,
Make worlds out of souls, universes
Drowning in metallic wine; the swollen eye,
A blackened olive, a stillborn rosebud.

Nothing beats the stench of the sun.
It beats the stale shadows, snuffed out before
Becoming late summer locusts; like laughter
at a funeral, slipping through the lines, silver hair
Falling everywhere the light touches,
A bloodless disease, unaborted.

Run while you can, while your crutches are still
Clean, while the bluebells are still sleeping.
Run before the clock stops, before
The aching of your chest dims, your voice
shedding its skin, dancing, an electrified doll
At the children's birthday party.
Their shrill
Innocence cures nothing.

How the wind spins – Keon Wong (he/him)

i.

How the wind spins its last winter threads;
How sour the plums have become;
How empty, this home, this forgiveness.

ii.

God, that tantalising gaze
Of a dawn long awaited,
How painstakingly brilliant.

A pure orange pupil,
Manufactured into day

The memory of
butterflies leaving.

I butchered everyone at the warehouse – Keon Wong (he/him)

I replaced their names with numbers,
Patted them on the back, said good work
And sent them off to dispatch.

Just the other day
They were talking about being slaughtered.
They were laughing at it.

"What's a child going to do with 200 thousand?"
"What's the mother going to do?"
The government will take care of that.

The numbers are up, stacking like cold limp boxes
Across the hallways. The shrill rumble
Of metal dancing to manufactured suns;

Call it happiness—call it a hard day's work
That drops dead by midday.
Fill your skull with prayers that you're too busy to mean.

Love thy neighbour, love them so much
That they now live in your stomach.
One for many—money makes curious inventions.

Never start a letter with a why:
They never get it—not when their hands
Are always feeding another mouth.

Stuff them full with sweat and blood, nothing wasted; serve
Our time to obsolete gods
Like a delicacy.

Or perhaps, don't sell
Your children the dream of different plates
To the same platter.

It's normal – Keon Wong (he/him)

The slope is getting steeper,
And the stones—how marvellous,
They fall as if in harmony.

And to us, foolishly smiling,
Hanging onto the last twig;
Still, arms aiming for the sun.

Sagan. – Paloma Mckim
(she/her)

'Why didn't you stay over the other night?'
The question came from a stack of books and coats.
There was a wrong answer, honed to see if I could repair the
damage I didn't know I caused.
'I felt like I needed alone time, are you upset?'
'You really didn't realise it was embarrassing?
I had friends over, I was introducing you.
I think you knew,
When they said goodbye you were meant to stay at mine, you
changed your mind.
I don't know what they thought,
It looked like you didn't want to be with me.'
'I wasn't trying make things awkward.'
'Maybe you didn't mean to, but you did.'
I was tired, my reserves were low.
'I did?'

'You did.'

The words hang,
To come to some inevitable meaning:
I was wrong,
I'm wrong.

In the dilution of my defenses you become everything again.

'I'm sorry.'
For what?

'Thank you.'
For what?

'Thank's for being mature about it. I trust you so much.'
So much
that I can
deny your reality,
Leave,
belittle you,

Still, there is no question of the same thing happening in reverse.

You pick up the remote.

'What do you want to watch?'
'I don't mind'

'Thank you again.'
'For what?'

'Thank you.'
For what?
For repairing your idea of me:
A deluded reflection
of you.

Nausea – Paloma Mckim (she/her)

There is a moment for every party, at any party,
where being alone is needed.
the air where thought can recollect and social anxiety is deseeded.

I stepped outside for this precious pause, soon interrupted.

A six foot something with nail polish on one hand corners me
with a well-worn point he intended to be profound,
He pushed into my hand a slim volume of pages,
Bukowski: Women
He spoke to my grimace that his company invoked:

'You must understand Bukowski did not hate women,
He just hated what was beautiful. It confronted him with his
Ugliness.'

'Right.'
I replied,
My lack of interest, hard to disguise.

'Quite tragic...when you think about it.'

I did not think about it,
The point was undeserving of thought,
only adding to a sense of late-night nausea.

He looked at me with eyes that thought they had seen me.
But he couldn't see me at all
not at all, not at all.

Overheard – Paloma Mckim (she/her)

''It's hard to say,
to put nothing into words.
I understood it last night.
broken biscuits digging into carpet,
everything slouching to the floor.
On the side of the sink, so much on the plate was
untouched,
Two grilled tomatoes produced a
glazed over stare.
This is the total.
This is a particular way of being afraid.''

Silverleaves *(Banksia integrifolia)* – Karen E Fraser (she/her)

A bleak exaggerated sky downpours uninvited
upon our much-needed change of scenery.
Hour after hour we play waiting-games,
itching for corner-store coffee hot with hope
to change the tide of caged delirium.

We walk through breaks in clouds to sooth
our lethargy and windblown squints collected
as we lean into the turmoil storms left
littering the shoreline, muddy waves
frothing the edges of protected tea-tree dunes.

The curve of Earth becomes steep where ridges
of grassy hillocks ringbark secluded laneways,
each lined with an ancient, heavy overhang
of silver-tongued banksias, beautiful canopied
elders shaking out endless flutters of confetti,

draping the neighbourhood with their glitter
of quiet—the weekend locals dead-ended here
carefree and rippling with laughter, unaware
we invent stories of how they made good,
sneaking sideways glances of their longed-for lives,

thieving glimpses through open doors, inside
an old shed lumbered with a fallen painter's art—
forgotten canvases patinaed by a coverlet of dust,
colours of the lost and found—time stretching
as we breathe the lightning-fresh air.

there is an ocean of salt-damp, precious goodness
gracing us and this wild and woolly haven.
we are returned to our senses, nourished
by the ease of being together, gently
at home and deeply, even sweetly, at peace.

Confetti – Karen E Fraser (she/her)

frost sugar-coats a humble landscape.
leftover yester-blush peels slowly to reveal
the sun spotlighting a scattering of white

herons—confetti resting quietly in eucalypts,
quite unwilling to throw wings wide
against a bracing dawn that will break

their coats of icicles formed overnight,
frozen feathers of jewelled stalagmites ready to plink
into cold, dark waters birthing misty pillars,

offerings to a cloud-salted dome of sky, bursting
in clear hues of breathless blue as the whole
world of my body breaks open with causeless joy.

Two loads made it to the line – Karen E Fraser (she/her)

two loads made it to the line and back
in time to fold the warmth of tender breeze and
sunlight into their wefts and weaves.
linens strung at length beside heady Erlicheer
now stowed with fragrant hope till needed.

I find myself contented, knowing that simple acts—
    which return the simmer of introspection,
    the inward seasons of the hearth that look
    toward clearings alive with growth—
have made good use of sodden, fallow
empty glades and weeping, seeping corners
silent with promise, to become rich again
with arresting wildflowers and the goodness of intention.

to my mind, this is the way of it.
the shifting arc of sun that courts us to trust again
as blank canvases of winter burst forth
with all the colours of creation,
primped and primed for months of
ride and glide that end with gentle slide
inside dormancy, readying for rebirth.

remember stealing every shard of bright to tuck
inside bones aching for juicy and rejoicing,
our sun-star's fiery apex glazing every sky?

remember revelling in rich carpets of royal colours
falling gracefully as nature takes a final curtain call and
bows so deep our feet are lost beneath her skirts?

remember resisting the breathless monochrome of winter's blast,
fingers curled round noses bitten violet by relentless cold,
everything frosted with jewels and crushed pearls of left-over light?

remember welcoming kind, new shoots in every shade of green
signalling our re-emergence from sepia rooms, still
filled with one long breath exhaled by candlelight?

what we are searching for is right here, where we are
grateful for laughter, for loving
and even lamenting each passing season

so, hold dear this inbuilt longing to reach toward the light and
celebrate your baskets full and empty nonetheless,
honoured to play a part in every scene remaining,

clean and warm and nourished and blessed enough
to be returned daily—free tickets in hand to every wondrous show
and a fortune in blessings and new beginnings
pouring into every pocket.

Mariana, she is keeping them – Karina Fiorini (she/her)

the minutes gurgle like the dying breaths of an old telephone line
strange tongues of men and women and women and men
lap hypocrisy into hollow echoes
what do they say? morals are no corals, rising
voices mute the blooms of the ocean
in tandem to ruined skylines above social eyes
like acid rain around a spool of tattered words
unsheltered, trees and reefs are dead
their ashes follow a cremation ceremony, then buried
in the deepest trenches of Mariana,
she is keeping them, for the next generation
as yet await their terms of reference
to pick up the phone once again, echo intimate artifices,
mend frayed oxygen memories
time keepers of fresh truths.

A Codependent Diagnosis – Daphne Fauber (she/her)

I've been meaning to ask my therapist;
Can you give your gut biome an eating disorder?
Or does the DSM-5 only diagnose planets and not its citizens?

If my microbes influence
my thoughts
my hopes
my dreams
am I off the hook for
all the times I
fucked it up?

Or are we both responsible
for every misstep
bad joke
late flight
a Pincer Maneuver
towards regrets
and hurt feelings?

In a positively negative feedback loop
of predetermined pain
we have survived
in spite of the combined effort of
my ancestors
my forefathers
my microbes
myself
with a short lifetime of accolades.

A Nobel prize in PTSD with
a certificate in anxiety
and a double major
in executive dysfunction
and disordered eating
with a perfect four point GPA.

Don't you know?
Generational trauma transplanted
across species
across bloodlines
across lifetimes
is an academic achievement
your parents can be proud of.

To Sylvia – Daphne Fauber (she/her)
A response to Sylvia Plath's 'Mushrooms'

The door is wide open
and we spread on the wind,
a certain disposition,
—Infectious.

Minuscule yet suffocating
a shroud of
traveling,
swaying,
drifting,
entropy.

So very tired,
yet there's work to be done,
and so many of us!
How many of us?

Little or nothing,
voiceless, bland-mannered,
we nudge and shove
in spite of ourselves.

I fear we won't
see morning.

tagetes patula or back to school szn – nat raum (they/them)

you taste like marigold dirt, like acid
in freshly tilled soil churned with a
garden spade on a too-hot morning
in may—the time of year your mother

planted petunias and tomatoes for the
summer, the latter never harvested
and former barely bloomed before slugs
and hornworms arrived. by the by,

i've never made a habit of carrying
summer into fall, but i can't help
but remember hanging out of stone
gatehouse windows in seersucker,

wondering how sixty-six degree days
became the standard by which i
determine perfect, in human warmth
and in september weather.

poem tacked to the Adventurer's Guild bulletin board – nat raum (they/them)

After Stardew Valley

under the red clay of the valley's
soil, there has to be something, some
sort of reward besides muddy water
for my repeated shovel-strokes.
i legally require a tangible something

to stop the steel as it upends the
depths of dirt, grains flailing through
autumn air into a pile, skyscrapers
high—to cup in my stiffening fingers
as sunlight quits the sky and i guide

myself homeward with only moonlight
across the facets of an amethyst cluster.

herba viridis – nat raum (they/them)
After Resident Evil 4

at eighteen, i eroded my palms layer by layer
each time i climbed onto the back of el gigante,
swollen with *plagas*, and frantically mimicked
leon kennedy's precise knife cuts with my control
stick. i, bandaged like a martyr, would and never
learned not to ruin my hands in youthful vigor,

nor how to stomach the bitter of burdock
on its own, only soaked in wine with herbs
and orange zest. i still find shelter in the folds
of a temperate forest, in a pixelated shearling
jacket or thrifted flannel shirt hanging across
my shoulder blades; i still await the mysterious
green herb that blots out the wounds,
no questions asked.

self portrait as a queer demon icon – nat raum (they/them)

i was a god before i begged
my bones not to snap like twigs
underfoot when i fled, shrouded

by the shag carpet of stout firs.
i swelled too big for my white
gown in greed, only lusting

after the love of every man
i encountered, believing it
limitless. i was a god with a

dick bigger than anyone's,
spoon-fed my divine body
with a faceless fuckboy's

admiration. i ran from the state
of the swelling like a landmine
after sucking even the idea

of wanting boys dry as brush.

eroding – nat raum (they/them)

bruiseblue, i fold my hands and my
knuckles throb in sync into each other's,
sinew, the guts behind tumbled shell
still not so malleable as they are
forgettable; not so kneaded by

my barest nightmares anymore as
sparring with the ghosts of their grip.
how much of living is sifting ashes
through the sieve of moth-shredded
organza curtain between me

and the clarity i seek? which way
do i travel to leave behind my body
and all it's seen and heard? and
how many holes in shell or silk
is enough to see through?

Mistletoe – Kanishka Kataria (she/her)

Under the shade of what is said,
The mistletoe.

Branches, leaves, and twigs,
I craved for my life,
The mistletoe.

Where lies the broken shattered fancies
Of the fairytale which strived in bliss,
I craved for my life,
The mistletoe.

Bereaved of the tremor which once shook,
I craved for my life,
The mistletoe.

Beneath the shadow stays the starving,
With the memories of my first craving,
The mistletoe.

That Christmas did not feel festive,
That symphony did not whisper in harmony,
That star did not shine,
That almighty was not benign.

For my mistletoe
This Christmas, it is all in the snow.

It is written in the stars,
The strings we've fabricated so far.
Your voice still echoes in back end,
Your duskily visage still haunts in repentance.

Mistletoe, your K is still holding
The breaths in the lone painting.
For my masterpiece who is still alive
In the dark nights where rain patters to revive,
Under the shade of what is said,

Mistletoe.

FICTION

Her Best Friends, The Parakeets – Michael Gigandet (he/him)

The little girl liked her mother's parakeets. They sang happy songs to her from their cage high above her head.

She was not old enough to go to school, and because she and her mother lived in an old farmhouse in the country, there were no other children nearby to play with. Her mother never spoke to her in more than three words at a time, and those words did not count as conversation. The birds were her only friends. Their names were Petey, Rosie, Winnie, and Minnie, and each one of them was a different blend of colors with one sheen being more dominant so that she could easily tell them apart.

Petey, the shiny blue one, was the friendliest of the bunch. He never pecked at her hand when she reached into the cage while standing on top of the kitchen counter. Petey liked the way she rubbed her finger down the back of his head to his tail. The little girl could tell because he cooed and whistled while she petted him. "You are my especialist friend," she would tell him.

The others flapped their wings and thrashed around whenever she approached the cage. Her mother never let her pet the birds, so she had to wait until her mother took her afternoon nap after drinking too much of her medicine.

"Don't be afraid," she told the birds, but still they fluttered, little feathers floating from the cage until she trapped them. Gently holding their wings to their sides in her fist, her small fingers cradling the birds like a rib cage, she withdrew them from the cage and rubbed the back of their heads with her finger. She pretended that they were eggs so she would not grip them too hard.

"See," she said. "I'm not hurting you."

On the day she gave them a bath she held them under the kitchen faucet until they stopped squirming. After she lathered them with soap and rinsed them, she wrapped them in a paper towel like mummies to keep them from flying away and arranged them side by side on the counter to dry.

She walked to her mother's bedroom and stood at the door, listening to the fan whir, stirring the summer air over her mother, collapsed on the bed. "Mommy," she said but not loud enough to wake her.

When the little girl came back to the kitchen the birds were lifeless, their eyes hooded, vacant.

She picked up Petey, kissed him and said, "I will always love you."

When a Door Closes – Elizabeth Motes (she/her)

Sidra crouched by the windowsill with the wind tousling her hair and a gun in her hand. It was late now, just around midnight, and she knew her target would soon reveal herself on the street below. Still, she sat ready in case she arrived early, with the night air cooling her skin even as she kept her face pressed along the wall to keep hidden. Just a few more minutes, and then she could go home.

The city down below was as quiet as it could get. She could hear the distant sounds of traffic, cars driving and honking, occasional music, or sometimes an echo of laughter or yelling. She shifted her weight as she kept the gun aimed down toward the street. In the abandoned apartment where she waited, it was silent, save for the sounds of the city. From down below, she would be nothing but a shadow.

With such a late assignment, Sidra had hoped for a nice view of the sky, but the city lights hid every star. She couldn't even see the moon at her angle. That was one of her bucket list items—getting out of the city to see the stars. A camping trip, maybe.

But for now, she had to wait for Nora Blake to emerge on the street below so that she could get this job over with. She knew what to look for having studied Blake's photo to ensure there were no mistakes. Long, pale blonde hair, about five foot eight in height, likely dressed well, blue eye—though she wouldn't be able to tell from where she stood. Blake wouldn't be alone, but she'd been told that wouldn't be an issue. Sidra didn't have any details beyond that. The devil was in the details, and if Sidra let herself get caught up in them, it would be at her expense. She had no idea why Nora Blake had to die that night. But it didn't matter.

She was tempted to check her watch again, but not long had passed, and Blake was due to emerge any moment now, so she couldn't risk hesitating and missing her. Of course, she had no idea where Blake was coming from, but from the late hour and knowing that she wouldn't be alone, Sidra could guess that her last night had at least been a fun one. And that she and her friends would most likely be drunk—that was a plus. Though Sidra's escape plan meant that she could get out even if Blake's friends immediately spotted her and decided to avenge their fallen friend, she took comfort in knowing they would be too out of sorts to pursue her.

A creaking sound came from behind her. Sidra whipped around, gun in hand, to find Nora Blake quietly tipping the door shut behind her. The light from the window just barely illuminated her face, but Sidra would have recognized her by her blonde hair regardless.

"I'm unarmed," Nora said, holding her thin arms up in defense. She smiled softly, as if the situation was merely awkward and not dire. As Sidra had predicted, she was dressed finely in a thin, sleeveless white dress appropriate for the summertime. No shoes, though. She must have taken them off to sneak up on Sidra.

Sidra kept her gun pointed at her but didn't shoot. Things were now wildly off-script, and she had no idea if Nora had others waiting nearby.

Nora slowly lowered her hands. "What's your name?"

"Sidra." She wouldn't have the chance to tell anyone else.

"Sidra," she repeated, nodding. "I imagine you know who I am. Or at least I hope you don't go pointing guns at *complete* strangers." With her light hair and dress, she almost resembled a ghost. Or an angel.

Sidra stayed silent, listening for anything to indicate others were waiting nearby for Nora. Whatever game Nora was playing, Sidra had to get out of it.

Nora tilted her head to the side, waiting for Sidra to speak. When she didn't, she asked, "Do you know anything about me, Sidra?"

"That's not my business."

"What is your business?"

Sidra's eyes flickered to her gun, then back to Nora in response. Nora nodded. "I see." She stepped forward, and Sidra gave her a warning look. She held up her hands slightly as though to remind her she was harmless. "Did you ever think of doing anything else with your life?"

"Where are the others?"

"What others?"

"There were supposed to be others with you tonight."

Nora frowned slightly, her red lips tugging at her face, and shook her head. "I did have plans for tonight," she conceded. "But then I realized that there was no one really worth spending the last night of my life with. That sort of perspective tends to make you reevaluate your priorities."

Even at her explanation, Sidra wasn't going to count on her being alone. "How did you know I would be here?" She realized then that her night wasn't going to be over once Nora was gone. Now she would have to find Nora's informant, too.

"Does that matter?"

"It does to me. Who told you?"

"You're not much of a conversationalist, are you?" Nora asked, mostly to herself. "Straight to the point." She took another step forward, but Sidra didn't try to warn her off this time. Maybe her story was true and she was just trying to make some meaning of her final moments, not fight it. Still, she stayed on guard as Nora continued, "Who's more valuable? Me, or the person who told me you would be here?"

Bargaining. This was a game Sidra could play. She lowered her gun without loosening her grip. "If you give me their name, maybe we can work something out." Lying did make her feel somewhat guilty, but she needed that name.

Nora smiled. She held her hands together and said pointedly, "I'll believe that when you put the gun down."

"I'm not convinced that there aren't others hiding around here."

Nora considered her words, then lifted her foot and slammed it on the ground, once, then twice. Sidra pointed her gun toward her in automatic response. She continued stomping both her feet against the floor, sending the sound echoing through the quiet building.

She finally stopped and looked up at Sidra with amused eyes. "No one else is here." She lowered her gun again.

Nora let out a breath and wandered to the other side of the room, not any closer to Sidra. Her gaze traveled around the room, deliberate and slow. "I didn't have to come up here, you know," Nora said without looking at Sidra. "I could have called the police on the crazy woman with a gun in an abandoned apartment."

"I would have been gone by the time they got anywhere near here."

She lit into a smile. "That was exactly my thought. And I wouldn't want to inspire an angry assassin to come after me. I would much prefer a calm one." She took another few steps toward her, then stopped. She studied Sidra closely, with something gentle in her eyes.

"You're not a killer. You don't like it, I mean. I can tell."

"It's an acquired taste," Sidra deadpanned.

Nora didn't smile. "How much can I pay you?"

Sidra withheld a sigh. She needed to get them back on track of the informant. "It's not going to do you any good to put a price on your life."

"Not mine. Yours." Her stare was steady as she stepped closer to Sidra. "You could start a new life somewhere far away from here. Be whoever you want to be."

As if Sidra hadn't thought of that before. As if she hadn't been *bribed* before. No amount of money could clear away her past, not in any way that mattered.

"I can't just start a new life," Sidra told her, "when I have so many loose ends. Like your informant. The one who apparently knows my whereabouts."

Nora did smile at that. "Don't worry about him."

"Give me his name and I won't."

"Tell me a story. Then I'll give you his name."

"What story?"

"The story of how a nice girl named Sidra becomes an assassin," Nora said. "What drives her to kill when it's not in her nature?"

Bargaining, bribing, now this. Guilt-tripping. "Being a nice girl doesn't spare any lives," she said. "If I decide not to kill you so I can rest easy tonight, someone else will get the job done by morning. Sparing my feelings won't do anyone any good." At least Sidra made quick work of it. There were plenty of killers in the world, but not many nice ones.

"And what becomes of you in the end?" Nora pushed. "What's your reward for all the sleepless nights?"

She shrugged. It felt shallow to answer *money*, and money wasn't really what she was after—it was freedom, independence. A distant concept, but she had to believe it was within reach. Sidra answered, "Getting to see the sun come up the next morning, I guess."

Nora gave her an affectionate look, the light from the window making her already white face even paler. A vampire, Sidra thought. Nora also resembled a vampire. She nodded her head toward the window. "What if we just waited here," Nora suggested, "and watched the sunrise?"

She didn't need to check her watch to know, "It's several hours until sunrise."

"But it will be a very peaceful few hours."

Sidra glanced out the window, her gun hanging loose in her hand. She watched the scattered lights of a nearby hotel, listened to the sounds of traffic that had dimmed since Nora's arrival, felt the gentle breeze against her face. It didn't feel like a night where someone would die, but she knew enough to know that it never did.

The knowledge didn't stifle her surprise when Nora placed her hands on her back and shoved her out the window.

A short gasp, and then the air was no longer gentle, but racing against her as she fell.

Perfect Memory – Elizabeth Motes (she/her)

I need it to rain so I can see my mother.

She died ten years ago, when I was seven, from cancer. My memories from that time are mostly just blurs with a few vivid moments, like when it really hit me that Mom wasn't going to get better. My dad had brought home fast food that night, and I remember crying at the table with a half-eaten burger in front of me. The funeral itself was a rush of hugs and well-wishes, but I remember Dad and I sitting on our old living room couch and watching a movie afterward, both of us quiet and tired.

I don't even remember all the details of the first time Mom appeared to me after she died. It started around a year after her death. It was pouring that day, so I had to walk home from school gripping my umbrella close to me from the wind. Dad was still at work when I got home. I dropped my backpack on the ground and hurried to the backyard to let our dog inside.

And then Mom was just there. Not in her hospital clothes, like in my final memories of her. She wore one of her old sweatshirts and jeans with her blonde hair pulled into a ponytail. She turned to face me as if this was our routine, her waiting in the rain for me to come home.

I don't remember how I reacted. Knowing it, I probably cried, unless I was too caught off-guard. I know I didn't go back inside or even consider it. She was there. She was back. I didn't care how it was happening, not at first.

Mom can only visit when it rains. I once tried asking her why.

She shrugged. "It's just the way it is." The words were spoken gently. Just a mom trying to help her daughter understand a bizarre world.

All of her answers about the logic of it were just as vague. How she was there, what she knew about death, where she went when the rain passed. Maybe she didn't want to tell me, but I think she genuinely doesn't know. I try not to think about it.

Right now it's late July. It hasn't rained since the middle of April.

I'm lying down in the grass of my backyard and staring up at the cloudless sky with sweat prickling at my forehead. It's not as if I can expect a lot of rain in Arizona, of all places, or act surprised when we get less and less of it each year. I've tried different ways of summoning her throughout the years. Spraying our hose up in the air, for instance, or filling up my bathtub, as if the quantity of water has something to do with it. Dad thought it was all part of the mermaid phase I went through as a child. I don't think he questioned it much because he was just happy to see me engaged in something. We still visit the aquarium every summer because of it.

Years ago, we had a snow day, and I was so thrilled because I thought Mom would appear. She didn't, which I still don't think makes any sense since snow is literally frozen rain. I told her as much when I saw her next, and she didn't even try offering an explanation.

"Did you do anything fun with your snow day?" she asked me instead.

I told her about sledding with Dad, and the subject was dropped.

But I'm counting on it raining this summer because I won't be here in the fall. Even though I'm going to school farther north of home—meaning more storms—I don't think I'll be able to see her. It's tricky enough to find time to see her at home alone, and a lot of that depends on Dad working long hours. As far as I know, I'm the only one that can see her, but I don't know if that's my will or hers or neither. Our dog never even reacts to her. That's always bugged me.

I assumed it would rain sometime between April and now. I didn't say goodbye the last time I saw her.

It's a ridiculous thought. I've already gotten nine extra years with her, and there's no reason to think she won't be here whenever I visit home.

That's what's bothering me. I don't think she's real.

If she works with some kind of magic, then what are the rules? Only I can see her. And why rain? That's the heart of it all, right down to the amount it pours. When it drizzles, Mom's voice comes out in faint words and her skin is pale. In storms, she looks just as she did when she was alive and perfectly healthy, her laugh loud and cheeks rosy with joy.

You would think the rules sound like they were made up by a grief-stricken eight-year-old. It makes the most sense. I think I didn't know how to cope with the first anniversary of her death, so I imagined her in my backyard, and I've kept it up since because I don't know what else to do. That's why I think that once I leave for school, she won't appear again. I don't think she can survive the change.

I asked her once if she was scared when she was dying. I was worried she would dodge the question, but she didn't.

"I wasn't," she said. It was barely drizzling, but her voice came out steady and clear. "I had you and your dad with me. That was all I needed."

Grim topics aside, we've talked about everything throughout the years. We sit together in the wet grass and she listens, sometimes offering stories from her own life, ones that I remember her telling me when I was young. All the while, I try to ignore how her shadow doesn't appear in the growing puddles, how she manages to stay perfectly dry in the wet, or how she hasn't aged and simply appears the way she looked before she got sick.

There were long periods of time where I could forget all the fantastical elements of it. Sometimes I could almost convince myself I still had my mother in my life. But then the image of her lying on the hospital bed would flash in my mind, and no matter what I told myself, I had to reconcile that those were my real and final experiences with her.

A single cloud appears in the sky. Just a small puff of white. I watch it linger in its place. There won't be a storm today, or tomorrow.

Dad will be home from work soon. He had an early day and said he would bring home dinner. I get up, wipe the sweat from my forehead, and go back inside.

Soy Chicano – Jacob Teran (he/his/el)

The night is calm as I prepare for my first night drive. My mother's keys to her car are in my possession and she is fast asleep from a long day answering phone calls from single mothers on their child support claims. I just finished smoking some fine yerba that I had left over from putting ends in with the homies earlier. I am faded yet cognizant that I am about to break the law. I take a deep breath and make my way downstairs to our 5-garage carport after locking the black front door and patio gate behind me. I wait for the Santa Fe Train to pass just a block away from Olympic Boulevard to disguise the sound of me opening the garage and starting the car up. I learned from living upstairs that you can hear anything, from people conversating to people fucking in my garage, if it's quiet enough. Tonight, was yet another quiet night and I did not want to fuck this up for myself. The train makes its presence known as it hollers from a distance. I time it perfectly as the train shouts its iron lungs across the black sky. I slip the sliding lock from the garage and lift the ancient brown door, unlock and enter the slick black J30 and insert the key for the ignition. I reverse and take off in the black of night.

Before I make my way down my street, I must make sure I have some appropriate tunes. My mom has several CDs in her car but what music would she have that would suit a night like this? I turn on her portable CD player, which she mentioned her boyfriend installed a couple of weeks ago, to see what she was listening to, and I am immediately mesmerized.

As the CD player turns on, the man known as Rick James' "Give It To Me Baby" blares out from the stereo as if he is riding shotgun with me. I raise the volume up to a blasting point with the windows down as I drive down Sapro Street. At fifteen years old, as I drive down my street, I feel on top of the world. Among my homies, even the ones who were the dopest, even toughest, no one would have ever dared to steal their mom's car in the midst of the night. I am that kid from the block to do so. I drive slow to show off, just so the homies and neighbors can hear me bumping this funky shit that is not only new to my ears but also something I immediately dig. I have one destination in mind as I blast through the hits of my new favorite artist. The destination I am heading for is my Abuela's house in Boyle Heights. I navigate through the streets, making sure to stop at every single red light while keeping trucha por la juras. I finally got to Quiet Canyon—the city's golf course—to where the entrance of the 60-freeway is across the street. I have never driven on the freeway before, let alone driven alone, but here I am riding solo in my mom's black Infinity. Rick James is in the backseat and Curtis Mayfield is now in my passenger seat as he roars "Little Child Runnin' Wild" at the top of his lungs. Both the lyrics of Mayfield and driving on the 60-freeway bring back memories of driving with my mother to visit my Abuela when I was a morro.

It was around this point I began to question my own identity. I did not know Spanish at this time of my life, besides the slang, and I didn't even try for the fear that my accent was too "white." I knew I was Mexican but did not quite "feel" Mexican yet. I didn't feel I was American either, although I knew I was because I was born here. The term Chicano randomly popped in my mind, and I pondered on what a Chicano is, where I first heard it, and whether I was that or none of the three. Maybe I was doomed to walk the Earth as the dark-skinned pocho with no place to call home or identity to identify with. The mota must have been kicking in as I drifted in and out of my weird thoughts.

What the fuck was a Chicano? A legitimate question that was never quite answered in my barrio. You were either called a paisa, chunti, or indio if you really had indigenous features, or simply, a Mexican. But *what the fuck* was a Chicano? I didn't know. The earliest exposure of what a "Chicano" was or sounded like was when my mom would drive me to my Abuela's house in Boyle Heights and her dancing to Santana's "Oye Como Va." This Latin fused rock music perked my ears as I had never heard this type of music. It was not the typical American pop or rock music I heard on the radio, but it was not what would be considered Mexican music as I would occasionally hear from my Abuelos' neighbors. It was Chicano with an "¿Y Que?" attitude. Santana's intro to "Black Magic Woman" came on next and my mom was twisting her neck and head slowly as if she was in a trance. The energy that came from my mom must have been contagious because my neck and head started doing the same thing. As we came off the 60-freeway, she had this habit of letting go of the brake down the 6th Street hill. Both of our stomachs would turn and tickle as she would groove and shake her hips to Santana's guitar solos.

Every time we drove through Boyle Heights, it felt like a different world. The vibrant murals on the walls told stories of our proud Brown People. Street vendors would always be working in this urban jungle selling esquites, tacos, and ice cream, making an honest living to provide for their families. Families would work together to sell flowers and churros off the freeway exits. Taqueros worked diligently without breaks in the corners of streets with lines feeding empty stomachs to people of all ages. Ice cream trucks that kids would chase and shout to snack on chili lollipops, Lucas powder, and bubblegum ice cream. This was my scenery while we drove through her barrio where she grew up, all the while we'd listen to Santana.

When we parked on the crowded street of mi Abuela's, my mom would always remind me, "Do not forget to tell your Abuela, 'Hola, ¿como esta?,'" and, "te queiro.'" I never understood why I couldn't just tell my Grandma, "Hello, how are you, I love you." This was a cultural custom that no one could explain, not even my mother. It was something that my thirteen tias y tios would teach their own kids, as well as their sobrinos. It was the right thing to do and our moms and tias made sure we always executed our proper greetings. Pero, it also made me feel good when I greeted my Abuela in Spanish and the immense joy that crossed her overworked and wise face. My Abuela was a beautiful woman. She would always smile and show so much love to all of her grandkids. I almost felt proud of the words that I was taught to repeat by my mom and the surrounding family members, as if I was part of a tribe, because, well, I was. Mis tias, tios, primos, were all part of this living tribe of Chicanos. Not part of Mexico, nor part of the Estados Unidos. We were part of a tribe that was mixed with brown and white skin members that did not have a wholesome home to claim. A language that was not entirely Spanish, since my family threw in English words, but a language nonetheless that kept us linked.

I remember my Abuela being the matriarchal leader of our entire family. If she wanted a party to happen, mis tias y tios would make it happen. Mi Abuelo was pretty chill and would sit quietly in the sala watching boxing fights on the Mexican program channels. As children, I would play "tag" and drive not just our parents, but our Abuelos crazy from all the chaos we would create.

"Ryan, behave or you're going to get it!"

"Brian, put your uncle's beer down!"

"Chingao! Guillermo Andrew Hernandez! Stop running around the house! Now!" When you heard your full name, you knew you fucked up. Mis primos and I were notorious for running amok in our Abuelos' house.

Our Abuela never had to tell her kids anything of our misbehavior, just one sigh, and our full names would be summoned to a full jury and our crimes would be judged right then and there. Whether we ran around the house, threw lemons to nearby houses from Abuelos' Lemon Tree, our violations were given a verdict of misdemeanor or felony depending on the crime we committed.

When mis primos and I were all tired and calm in the evenings, my family was renowned for telling stories in la cocina. My family's stories would range from the people they encountered at their jobs, funny stories from the past when they were children, and the paranormal scary shit. The entire house would be dark and the only light in the house was within the "Kitchen Gathering of Stories." My family would mix English with Spanish when they told their stories, where I would try my hardest to follow but only get lost in translation. They would use "Como dice," to get their message across before adding the English word they could not interpret. Abuela y Abuelo would simply nod their heads in agreement whether they understood the English words mis tias y tios would use. Usually one of my primos, tias, or tios would tell me what they're talking about but probably one of the most complex and memorable stories is how my Abuelos got here to Boyle Heights.

I can recall in one of these gatherings of story-telling of my Abuelos and their classic historia romantica of meeting before they became accustomed to the Estados Unidos. A story of how a man woos a woman to his grasp and takes the woman away from the confines of her family, with of course, the approval and acceptance of the parents. Mi Abuelo instantly fell in love once he set eyes on my Abuela. A beautiful story of how two individuals that had little to nothing due to economic circumstances found love. The intriguing aspect is that both mis Abuelos were born in Arizona and did not know each other until they both coincidentally moved back to Jerez, Zacatecas. Apparently both my Abuelos' families were from the same state in Mexico—what are the odds of that happening? Once they met, it was not very long until mi Abuelo asked for Abuela's hand in marriage. They were madly in love and had their first children, the oldest tia y tio, but according to the legends, living in rural Mexico was difficult to raise a family the way they wanted. The burden of poverty and lack of medical benefits along with healthcare made it evident to my Abuela that if a family was to be sustained, they would have to move to where she and her husband were born, the land of opportunity as some say—the Estados Unidos.

Of course, mis Abuelos had a clear understanding of moving away from their homeland in Mexico, yet their home country lacked the security they needed to raise a large family. This was not to undermine the orgullo they had of their motherland. Somewhere along the journey of falling in love, trying to make a life in Mexico had faltered, and they "realized" their life was not meant to be in Mexico. They wanted something more for themselves, not just for them, but for their children they were to bear. A belief that I feel most Mexicans have when immigrating to a land that was rightly their own once upon a time. So, mis Abuelos assimilated, because they were "good citizens." Citizens that caused no problems. Citizens that respected authority because if they rebelled, they were "indios," "savages," that had no sense of dignity and pride to one's country—propaganda that I later learned was taught to assimilate "new" people to this country. They were American and no one could take that away.

"So what if we spoke Spanish and not English," mis Abuelos thought, "we gained legalization the way this country wants it. We were legal. If we wanted to own a house like the Jewish family down the street, we could. Or like the Japanese that earned their income to purchase property next to us, why not us?"

Like my grandparents, African American, Jewish, Japanese and many other ethnic groups dirtied their hands to cement their place in a country that promises equal opportunities to those that work hard enough. Boyle Heights was that place of opportunity to mis Abuelos, and they took that opportunity to their advantage. Because of their ganas, orgullo, and willpower, they were successful and did so without complaints or help from the government.

I returned back from my time capsule of the past to reenter the ship of the present. My journey was that of a brown kid who didn't know Spanish, had no identity, and learned how to act as a model Mexican-

American citizen to my society. I was called "mayate,"—the equivalent of the n-word by kids in school, on my block, and by some primos of my own because of dark skin. I despised this word, the older I got for it was not only meant as a derogatory toward African American people, but also because it was a hatred for my skin color that I later learned to love. I also learned from some of mi gente that "indos" or "paisas" were "low-class" Mexicans who only spoke Spanish and were to be avoided at all costs. Many of my family members told me that these "lower-class" Mexicanos were "ghetto" and were drunks living off government funding—another false stereotype I later learned was not true. Even at that age, I felt something was off when I heard those things. II liked listening to and dancing to cumbias, and when I had a good buzz, I was proud when people heard my grito, for it was not half bad. But I was a "TJ" for doing these things—another derogative for "low-class" Mexicans referring to those that reside on the border of Tijuana.

So who the fuck was I then? I was a brown being that was called fucked up names because of my dark skin by some of my own people. Who knows what white people thought of me when they saw me, but that's beside the point. This is how I felt. I still sometimes feel this way. I was supposed to speak better than the light skinned kids and the darker ones or else I was a foreigner, an n-word, or a dumb pocho to the ignorant and mislead.

These thoughts all come crashing in like a tidal wave as I pass East Los Angeles into Boyle Heights territory.

I am living in a foreign world that remains obscure to me. I cannot relate nor feel like I belong; I feel as though there is something missing, something there that I cannot explain. Am I the only one who feels this way? Suddenly, I feel that I truly may be alone in this ephemeral experience as I grasp the steering wheel. Maybe I'm tripping from this yesca. I approach the exit of the 60 freeway onto the 6th street exit, the same exit I remember driving down while listening to Chicano sounds with my mom.

Rather than going down 6th street, I turn left on South Lorena Street, then turn right on Olympic Boulevard—the street that can take me back home to Sapro Street. The streets are empty. Graffiti of both the White Fence and Evergreen gangs are littered throughout the area to let people know where they're at. The placasos on the wall were the GPS of the time. You can never get lost if you knew what gang belonged to the area you were in, and if you didn't know, well, ni modo. As I approached Olympic Boulevard westbound, I knew I was heading into what is known as VNE territory—Varrio Nuevo Estrada. The Estrada Courts are a low-income housing area at the end of Boyle Heights, an area my family never drove by, but mostly because there was no reason to. I drive cautiously as there are dudes all around the area. The shadows out this late could be homeless or folks up to no good. The last thing I need is to run into some vatos locos or the pigs, driving my mom's car, I mean, driving my mom's stolen car. I lower the music since I am growing a little paranoid due to the weed and area I'm in. I take a turn towards the Estrada Projects and drive slowly as the road becomes narrow and darker from the trees partially covering the streetlights. My mom's car being all black with slightly tinted windows and my nearly bald head are suspicious enough and yet, here I am, high, creeping through the VNE Projects.

From my driver's side, three shadows appear out of thin air from the dark project building. They walk quickly to my side and without thought, I stomp on the brake pedal by accident making my car come to a complete halt—an unintended message that probably screamed I wanted pedo. Quickly realizing what I have done, I hit the gas pedal.

"Wasup fucking bitch!!" "Barrio Nuevo Gang!!"

I can barely make out what they shout but I don't stick around to find out. I hunch my head over just a bit to see where I'm driving, with fear I might be shot from behind. I smash down the Estrada Courts with shadows appearing from the surrounding dark corners of the projects and overcrowded trees. I finally come out of the projects and turn left on 8th Street hauling ass without looking to my right. I almost t-bone an oncoming SUV. The SUV honks and swerves to the next lane as I keep looking back to see if I am being tailed. My heart is thumping. Sweat drips from my brow as I head down to what I now see in front of me, Downtown Los Angeles. I turn right down South Soto Street and turn into a residential street and pullover, parking with my headlights off. I chill for about 10 minutes sitting in the cockpit of what I thought would be my coffin. I take a deep breath and laugh at what just took place. I trip out and think "what the fuck am I doing driving around Boyle Heights at 1am?" I laugh off my pendejadas as I come back to my senses. I'm lucky I haven't got stopped by la juras or caught slipping by VNE, although I almost did in the Estrada Courts.

"Fuck it. Time to go home," I say aloud as I turn on the headlights.

I wanted to drive to mis Abuelos house, stop there and reminisce further, but I think I had enough fun for the night, plus, I only know so much of Boyle Heights and don't want to get lost completely. I turn back to Soto and know I'll eventually run into Olympic which will take me back home. I try to keep my composure and not drive suspiciously as I drive near the Estrada Courts again. I turn and drive down Olympic, and I can't help but notice the murals on the large Estrada Court buildings, admiring the art of what I thought was Chicano art at my tender age. I proceed down and see a figure on a large wall that looks like Che, which I have seen on shirts, stickers, and flags across swap meets I have been to many times with my dad. The area looks clear, no cars behind me, and no shadows in the distance, fuck it. I pull over to get a better look.

A painted longhaired man points at me with eyes that pierce right through my soul. Giant letters that form a message to the left of his face read, "We are not a minority!!" I feel this immense pride reading that and digest what it means. I stare at Che as he stares right back at me. I feel a bit less alone in my feelings as to who I am or can identify as, as I repeatedly read, "We… We…" I feel a sense of power to the statement asserting "what we are not." Perhaps, others like me have driven through Olympic to see this mural of Che and feel a sense of belonging.

I didn't know if Che was a Chicano at this point in my life, but it didn't matter to me. I felt refreshed and proud and could not entirely explain how or even why.

I put the music back on to calm my nerves and I make my way down Olympic. A song comes on and the intro sounds sort of like Santana but at the same time, different. Suddenly I hear the same repeated lyrics that further fortify my identity. El Chicano's "Don't Put Me Down (If I'm Brown)" blares on the car speakers, and I wiggle my neck and head all the way down back home.

Nightmares – Dani Solace (they/he/she)

My arms seem to move on their own these days. Control slips away as I pull at my scalp. Skin gives way quickly, alarmingly frangible. My fist pushes through bone to grasp at my brain in handfuls. It disgusts me, but I cannot stop. *Why can't I stop?* It's soft and flimsy in my hands, under my fingernails, *why is it so warm?*

All at once, I snap out of my trance. Trying to open my bedroom door seems impossible with the weight on my limbs, but I manage. After making it to the bathroom, I begin examining my reflection. Though my skull is still intact, I am...off-kilter. A strange feeling washes over me, followed by an unfamiliar taste. Something...

Something drips out of my ear. Am I going mad? *I must be.*

Tilting my head, the evidence of my sanity becomes clear. A nightmarish substance gushes out of my ear and down the back of my throat. Something bittersweet and metallic invades my senses, jarring me to the bone.

Rarely has such putridity plagued me. Rust and rot follow me into the real world. It's a wonder I did not vomit upon waking.

Finally free, I am left heaving. Nearly tripping myself in a rush to see the damage, there was none. All was silent, the winter night still young. The aftermath of that horror lay only in me.

Hours of searching for some understanding have brought me nothing. It seems my imagination overtakes me. How long will I grapple for peace?

Daylight brings relief, but not enough. Anxious to forget the visions of last night, I wade knee-deep in pages that will hopefully hold my secrets.

Weariness and fear creep in as dusk approaches. Try as I might to fight it, I am no match for my humanity. Whatever sleep shows me, I will stay vigilant. Though my body is weak, I still have my mind. Standing before a mirror once more, I am overwhelmed by the urge to push two fingers into the flesh of my shoulder. Ever compliant, I obey my fragile mind. My hand reaches so deep it unsettles me to meet no resistance. To see no blood. Even in my subconscious, I cower before the unnatural. I can no longer run from my instincts. From myself.

I have seen many gruesome things in the depths of my fitful rest. Through all the lingering themes of unease, this is recurring. I wish it did not feel like reality.

Could this be my doing? Or is some larger force at play orchestrating my unwinding? Pushing my mind to conjure things beyond terror is an unimaginable punishment. The aftertaste of spinal fluid still lingers today. Never can I hope to forget the warmth of brain matter between my fingers, coming apart in gooey chunks. When will it end?

When will it end?

Let Us Walk to Him – Deron Eckert (he/him)

The moon is bright, and our hands are full. We do not fear these woods tonight. He will not excuse our absence, and we would not dare ask Him for forgiveness. Forgiveness is for the catering chorus, not the silent, the ones who mouth the lulling hymns but seek more than can be offered from a pulpit.

The reward is great, so we carry not just what we can spare but all we have. The lesser among us tote mere packs, but those of means are burdened with heavier loads on carts pulled by mules. The uninitiated brought horses that had to be hitched at the threshold of thorns and are towing their trunks through damp earth, but it is no matter. If He had wanted horses, the arches of barren rose bushes would have hung high. The mules will suffice.

It would be impossible to pass through the tunnel of gnarled branches without the solitary ember that shepherds us forward. The naive fear the flame, recalling many who followed it in search of hope or gain only to find ruin, but the light before us once walked beside us. She knew then, as she knows now, He would not lead us astray. We know, too.

As we draw near to Him, the mules resist, sensing what lies before them. We are one and thrust the carts into their rears. When one falls and refuses to be persuaded by our motivations of foot and hand and stick and rock, he succumbs to the saw of a dull blade, his new smile gushing as he is dragged by a rope tied around his hooves. The other does not notice he is pulling the weight of his brother behind him. Let those who cannot walk be led, and please, let Him not be angry that we have spilled what was His.

The light reaches the end of the tunnel before us and spreads until the only thing that remains dark in the meadow is the tree at the center of the trees. This is His tree. He will be here soon. We must prepare. The hour is almost upon us.

One by one, we lay ourselves bare. We free ourselves of the ties that bind us to this place, our homes, and those who parade as family. We do not need them. He will save us from such lowly concerns and allow us to transcend. But first, we must give Him all we have.

The cold are stripped of their unraveling clothes, the hungry of their food, and the chaste of their veil. The stubborn mule is untied and placed carefully in the nook of His tree. Cornered, the companion kicks, spits, and snarls but is brought down with the same blade plunged into its rib cage with just as little effort. There is no light within the maw, and we must wait until the back of our hands feel the wet decay below them before nestling the fresh carcass atop it. It makes no sound as it settles because all that can be heard within is what sounds like the roaring, rapid clicks of cicadas.

We step back and wait for confirmation that we have offered enough, but the silence insists on what we have left to give. Our hands are stained red with the blood we let, except for hers. She dares not ask us if she must. So, with the sincerity of laying milk before a kitten thirsting for a dead mother, she places her love in His tree as her only begotten son cries for familiar arms and then no more.

The Skies are Made of Diamonds: – Supravo Rahman (he/him)

Lucy was on cloud nine. She floated upwards, stretching her hands towards the blue ceiling of the sky. Ten, eleven, twelve—she counted the clouds she crossed, giggling the whole time. Her mother was calling her from below, but Lucy pretended not to hear. All her life, she had wanted to see the stars. Her mother's anger would pass.

Unfortunately, some cowboys happened to be passing by the house at that very moment. Hearing her mother yelling, they got out their lariats and lassoed Lucy down. She was pulled back to her house, kicking and screaming, and tied to the posts of her bed. When her father got back home, there wasn't a lecture like she expected, but a promise that things would change.

The next day, her parents took her to the hospital.

"Her head is always in the clouds," they told the doctor, a pale thin man who peered at her from behind large circular glasses.

"What do you think, gentlemen?" the doctor asked his colleague, clearly flummoxed by the case.

"Her head is full of dreams," concluded the old man with the white beard. Rather jovially, too.

"Then the only solution is surgery," said the fat one, looking at Lucy like she was something good to eat, "We cut into her head and take the dreams out."

"No surgical procedure that advanced exists," interrupted the bald one, voice raspy like stone being dragged over ice, "I suggest we put her in cryostasis until our technology catches up."

"No need to be so extreme, gentlemen," laughed the blonde woman, twirling a lock of her hair with her forefinger, "It's nothing some therapy won't fix."

They argued for what seemed like hours. Finally, they made her a pair of iron shoes to wear.

"Iron is good," explained the doctor, adjusting his glasses, "It will ground you."

It did ground her. Physically, at least. Then the new family moved in next door and the son inevitably asked her what the shoes were for.

"It's so that I can't see the stars," she explained.

"What are stars?" asked her new friend.

She told him everything. All the myths that she knew. That high above the clouds, there existed millions of bright lights known as stars. Lights that sparkled like diamonds in the dark of the night. She even told him how there used to be a huge star called the sun, so big that the entire world revolved around it.

"So...the skies are made of diamonds?" he asked.

"Yes."

"If you ever see them, can you bring one for me?"

"I'd bring one for you right now if I could."

His face brightened. They snuck into his father's tool shed, and after an hour of experimenting with various power tools, managed to cut through the iron. Lucy immediately ran out, shooting for the sky. The dreams had been gathering in her head ever since she started wearing the shoes, and now they all sent her flying at once. She broke through all the layers of the clouds, and finally touched the vault of the heavens.

It was even more beautiful than she imagined. A kaleidoscope made up of millions of lights, twinkling and shimmering like fireflies against the dark blue tapestry of the sky. Lucy reached for the closest one. She thought it would be cold, like the diamond on her mother's wedding ring, but it was hot, very hot.

Before she knew it, she was falling. The winds roared in her ears, and the clouds shot up past her as she dropped. Her palm was burning, but she did not let go of the star. This, she would take home.

"Lucy is that you?" asked a familiar voice.

She had woken up in the backyard of her neighbours' house, and the boy was looking at her. There was something different about him though. He was taller, his hair was less messy, and he wore glasses.

"Where have you been?" he asked, "It's been years!"

"What are you talking about? I just left. Look, I got you a star."

She opened her charred palm, revealing the star to him. His eyes widened with shock, then narrowed with scepticism.

"That's not a star, Lucy," he said with a sigh, "That's just a ball of luminescent gas."

Born, Not Made – Danila Botha (she/her)

When I was a teenager, I didn't think I'd live to be twenty-one. I didn't know why, to be honest. It was just a premonition that felt true. I didn't get through things by imagining that one day I'd create some art from the experiences. I survived thinking, one day I'll be able to buy a shovel big enough to bury all of this in someone's backyard, and I'll never have to think about it again.

I blocked a lot of details from my mind, so when I go back and try to recall them now, there are blanks, events and chunks of time that are missing. I wonder if I'll ever get them back. I wonder if I want to. Before we moved to Canada, my mom had told me that she was moving for my sister Taryn and I, for our futures, for our safety. She'd wanted to do it all along, we knew, but my dad wanted her to stay. Then my grandparents were in an armed robbery in their house. It was seven at night, still light outside, and they were eating dinner in their kitchen. No one was killed, but they were hit and kicked and shoved under the table. My mom says my skin is as soft as my grandma's, we both bruise like peaches. They had to be quiet unless one of the guys was asking them where their valuables were. When we got there, hours later, the drawers were all emptied out, there were crushed lipsticks and feathers from duvets and pillows, torn apart. There were clothes on the floor, plastic hangers snapped in half, a sunhat crushed by a heavy shoe. My eyes couldn't take in all the chaos; my grandparents were always so fastidious, obsessive even, about cleanliness.

It was my job, my mom told me, to be well adjusted. It was going to be harder for my mom than it was for us. She was a well liked and respected doctor. No one would know her in Canada. Taryn was little, and I was young enough, she reminded me. Kids were resilient, everyone knew that. But bouncing back when you don't know the social codes or rules, when you have nothing in common with people, is basically impossible. I learned to fake it around my mom.

Once a week, on a Friday night, we would all have dinner together. She'd ask me how my day was, and I'd say fine, and she'd move on to Taryn, who was more expansive. Taryn instantly made friends. Taryn's teachers thought she was adorable. If my mom asked who my friends were, I'd tell her about my favourite characters in the books I was reading. She believed me, but then my memory for details was excellent, and her interest in me was always superficial.

On the weekends, my sister would get together with friends. Taryn had always been sweet and funny but back home she nearly constantly threw tantrums, bashing her baby teeth up into her gums when we played hide and seek, going headfirst into a wall at one of my birthday parties. She was the world's pickiest eater, something my mom used to complain about endlessly, but now, she thought I was the difficult one.

There was a girl, Yvonne, who was a year older than me who'd immigrated from Johannesburg at the same time. We'd gone to different schools, but we kind of knew each other. She was one of those obsessively normal people, someone who could pick up the trends and expressions and blend in, the kind of girl no one would ever be able to pick out of a line up. I was so jealous of her.

Yvonne walked with confidence. She lost her accent faster than me. I had to work at it. I watched a lot of bad American sitcoms about families who loved each other and kids who had the time of their lives in high school, cheerleaders and jocks and class presidents. I repeated phrases over and over so they sounded natural. "Yeah, right. I hate her guts. Oh My God."

I wasn't a bad student, but unlike at home, I wasn't an exceptionally good one.

Everything was different. Math was harder. The books we read were less interesting. I'd read under my desk when the teacher wasn't looking. Only one kid noticed.

"Any good?" he'd ask me, and sometimes we'd talk about books. I wasn't used to being friends with boys. I found it hard to talk to him, though I always wanted to.

There was a boy named Erez who only ever talked to me in a slow, loud over-the-top South African accent that sounded slightly Texan. Our assigned lockers were beside each other, so there was no escaping him. He had thin, curly hair, a wide forehead, and wide-gaped teeth that his braces couldn't fix. He was obsessed with all the popular girls, making up songs that he would sing them, buying them expensive chocolate for Valentine's Day.

There were seven of them, including Ruthie, a girl whose sister Annie was already good friends with my sister. She came up to me one day and told me that my mom asked her to look out for me. A few weeks later we went to the mall together, ate French fries, and even took those cheesy photo booth pictures. I thought I'd finally made a friend. The next day, I put the photos up in my locker, like I saw everyone else do.

Erez grabbed the photo, tore it up, and threw it into the industrial sized garbage at the end of the hallway.

"Ruthie's my friend," I protested and Erez snorted. "No she isn't."

Later that day, in class I was so sure that she'd be upset with him, that when he told me, like he always did, that I was a loser with no friends, I looked in her direction, and said "Ruthie's my friend."

Erez looked at her and laughed like it was the best joke he'd ever heard. "Ruthie, you want me to tell her? Are you really friends with *her*?"

Ruthie fixed me with the same big smile she'd had on the first time we'd talked.

"Of course," she said, in an over-the-top cheery voice, "I'm everybody's friend."

Another boy, Judah, had a long, thin nose, beady eyes, and sharp looking canines. He scuttled like a rat in the hallways. Together, he and Erez made fun of me while everyone either ignored them or laughed along.

One day, our French teacher was absent, and a substitute did the attendance.

Instead of Lindi, she read my name as Linder. Linder Bumbum, instead of Lindy Buxbaum.

Judah thought this was hilarious. He led the whole class in a chant, "Buh buh buh buh buh buh, BUM," to the tune of Charge! Like at a baseball game.

The class would chant it, then look at me, and I would slide down in my chair, trying to disappear.

The teachers would look away, like they couldn't hear anything. I'd never thought about my ass being big before, but I started asking my mom to buy me bigger clothes and tying sweatshirts around my waist.

Judah would make kids playlists, individualized and thoughtful, which slowly made him more popular.

"Bum, I made you one," he said one day, and I was stupid enough to ask to hear it.

It had one song on it, which I'd never heard of, called Mr. Personality. I think it was from the 1990's.

Over the chorus, Judah sung his own version "They call her Lindi personality because she's so ugly"

Nathan stood behind him, laughing so hard he had to wipe his eyes. The worst thing happened at Zev Epstein's bar mitzvah. Even if you had no friends, you got invited, because everyone invited the whole class.

Every table had heavy centrepieces made of silver balloons and a heavy weight.

I ate chicken for dinner. I danced to ancient dance music, including the YMCA, and the Macarena.

In the passage that led into the party room were stacks of extra chairs, five or six heavy piles of metal, padded chairs. Everyone was inside unless they had to leave to go the bathroom.

Erez and Judah were waiting for me in between the chairs. One of them was holding extra centrepieces, the other one held me so I couldn't move.

I didn't scream, but even if I had, the music was so loud, no one would have heard me. I'm not sure they would have cared if I had. They used five centrepieces in all, tied my hands and feet, and the back of my hair to a stack. If I moved, I threatened to bring a whole stack of chairs down on me. I was around five feet tall, and each stack was over six feet, at least.

Nobody freed me. Eventually my mom came to pick me up. I watched the colour drain out of her face when she saw me trapped there. She used her car keys to cut the ribbons.

The school's principal said, "It happened on a weekend, not on school property, so there's nothing we can do."

My mom didn't offer to let me move schools, so I didn't ask.

She channeled her rage into changing my behaviour. "What did you do, she asked to make them make fun of you?"

"Let's make a list," she said, trying to be practical, "of all the things you can change and do to make kids like you."
I stopped talking for a long time. If I didn't say anything, no one could make fun of me.

When I got home, it was weird to have to start talking again, so sometimes I didn't. I chewed a lot of gum. I went online a lot. I talked into my sleeves.

"Teenagers mumble," my mom told anyone who asked. "It's totally developmentally appropriate."

I read a lot. I drew sometimes. I listened to music.

I spent my lunches either in the bathroom or in the school library. I read just about everything in their fiction section, from The Hobbit to Holocaust literature.

I got skinnier. I tried my hardest to disappear.

They say artists are born, not made. It's true that I was always a weirdo. It's true that drawing and writing were my favourite things to do as a kid. I like creating imaginary worlds. I had imaginary friends for way longer than was considered normal. It's also true that if none of these things had happened, they might have remained hobbies. When I lived to be twenty-one, I officially decided to make the most of my life. If I hadn't needed to become invisible for so long, I might never have needed any recognition.

Out of Her Mind – Abigail Kangas (she/her)

As soon as the door opens, I bolt into the closet to avoid being seen. I do this every time Lilian comes home, but today it's even more important. She's mad. I can't tell who she's yelling at yet, but I can hear crying.

"Would you stop?! You know who I am!"

"No, I don't!" she says, crying even harder. I can see her now, a little girl, who looks to be six or seven.

"I am your mother! Stop playing around, Ashlynn, or you'll be going to bed early tonight." I can tell how exasperated she is, but Lilian doesn't have a daughter. She's thirty-two, and has never been married, or been in a relationship long enough to have a child.

The little girl quiets gradually, and when she finally stops crying, she says, "My name is not Ashlynn, it's Eva, and I think you mixed me up with your own child. My mom's name is Helen, and my dad's name is Robert. I live on—" but Lilian cuts her off.

"Your name is Ashlynn, I am your mother, and your father died two months ago!" She screams the last bit, and Eva starts crying again.

Suddenly, there's a knock on the door. It's probably the landlord, coming for the monthly check. Lilian is wide-eyed but walks toward the door. "Go sit in the living room, Ashlynn."

She opens the door, "Hello, sir. Can I help you?"
When he comes in, I see that it's a police officer. "Ma'am, we got a call a few minutes ago, saying that one of your neighbors saw something moving in here, and you weren't home yet.

Would you mind if I take a look around real quick?" He's already looking before she can nod her answer.

Doesn't he realize that there's something wrong with Lilian? She's a wreck, and it's only going to get worse.

I'm Jack, if you're wondering, and I died two months ago. I've been watching over her, making sure she's alright. I dated Lilian for two years. Before I died, she told me that I was the only man she ever loved. There is definitely something going on with her, though. She didn't used to be like this.

I always loved taking Lilian places, and spending time with her. She was a little uncertain of our relationship at first; she wasn't very open with her feelings. But after a while, everything seemed so natural.

But Lilian never wanted a child. She specifically told me that when I would bring it up, hoping she'd change her mind. I don't know where she found that little girl, but she seems to actually think her name is Ashlynn and that I'm her father.

After looking all through the house, he goes into the living room and sees Eva. She looks scared, so he sits down cautiously. "Hello. And who might you be?"

She just stares, and doesn't say anything, probably thinking that Lilian is going to freak out again if she says Eva.

"It's alright. You can tell me. What's wrong?" Nothing. "Can you tell me your name?" Still no answer.

He takes out his spiral pad and a pen and hands it to her. She takes it but doesn't write anything down.

Lilian comes in, carrying coffee. "What's going on?" she says suspiciously, looking back and forth between the two.

"Is this your daughter?" he asks, looking at Eva the whole time.

Lilian is silent for a moment. "Yes, of course, she's my daughter. Why else would she be in my house, on my couch?" she asks him defensively.

"Ma'am, she looks terrified, and there is nothing in this house that suggests a child lives here. I'm going to have to ask you to go stand in the foyer for a few minutes while I talk to the girl." He turns to Eva as Lilian walks away.

"Now, I want you to tell me your name, so we can get you back to your real parents. Can you tell me?"

She stays quiet for a moment and then says, "My name is Eva. My mom's name is Helen, and my dad's name is Robert. We live in a neighborhood called White Springs, and I was at the playground when she—" She looks up at Lilian, who is now crying. "She came over to me and picked me up, calling me her baby, like I was her daughter. I don't know her though, please help me." She talks so quickly he has to scribble to keep up.

"Okay, Eva. Do you know your parents' phone number? Or your address?" She shakes her head no.

"I'm sorry." She pauses. "I still get to go home, right?" She looks scared that he'll say no.

"Of course you do. I'll be right back." he tells her and walks into the foyer to talk to Lilian. "Can we go outside and talk?" he asks her, eyeing the door.

"Sure." She looks upset, like it really is her daughter who is about to be taken from her.

I don't know when I realize it, whether it was then, or when they actually take Eva, but Lilian really *does* think it's her own child. It's the way she looks at her, and I guess the police officer notices it too.

The officer left with Eva, and Lilian was put in a mental hospital to care for her, and to fix her. They said that she was experiencing a break from reality, caused by the loss of a loved one. They don't know about me, no one does, but they know that her dad died earlier this year.

She breaks down at least once a day, being trapped in a small room alone, aside from her once a day therapy session. Lilian is considered one of the more dangerous ones in this place.

I've visited her every day, and most days, I stay here all day. She's started talking to herself more and more frequently, which the doctors find concerning, but she's trying to talk herself through everything that had happened.

But then—well, then, she started talking to me, too. She told me she was sorry, that she loved me so much, that she wanted to see me just one more time, if that's all she could. She just wanted a chance to apologize, to make it up to me, what she did. I never speak back, but I listen, whenever she needs it.

About two months ago, Lilian was still grieving her dad's death, and I came over to her house to comfort her. She seemed to be telling herself that he was coming back, that he just went to the store and took a detour, that he got lost, that he was getting directions, on and on until I tried to tell her that he was gone for good.

Lilian had been my everything, so I wanted to help her feel better, to move on, even if she still missed him forever. But she shut down, stopped talking to me. And I know I shouldn't have, but I left. She kept telling me I couldn't help her and that I was worthless, that if she had been with her dad more instead of me, he would still be here.

I had given up on talking to her when I saw her walking in the park. Out of impulse, I went up to her, asked if we could talk. She tried to walk away, but I followed. She ignored me all the way back to her house, even when I tried telling her that I loved her, that I would always be there for her, that she could tell me anything she needed to get out of her system. But she slammed the door on me,

I could tell she wasn't okay, and I still had a key to her house, so I went in. She was in the kitchen, starting to make dinner. "Sit down." she said. I looked at her questioningly. She looked straight through me. "What are you waiting for?! I said sit!"

So, I sat. She rushed around the kitchen, banging pots and pans and gathering ingredients that made no sense together. I stood up.

"Lilian, are you alright?"

"I told you to sit down!" She was screaming at this point.

"Lilian, listen to me, Please, just talk to—"

"No! I said sit down! Stop telling me that everything is fine and that it's going to be okay, and that everything I'm feeling is normal! I lost my only living parent, the only person who ever cared about me! I! Am! Alone! But you wouldn't get it, because everyone cares about you! Just get out of my life!"

"Lilian, you need help. You can't live like this. I'll go if that's what you want, but then you would be really alone. I love you, Lilian. I always will, and I'm so glad I have you. I don't want to lose you. I need you." I'm crying but she doesn't seem to care.

She paused, silent, except for the sound of her breath hitching as she cried. "I love you too, Jack."

I moved toward her and wrapped my arms around her. We stayed there like that for a while, me just hugging her, crying, while I told her how much I love her.

I whispered, "He may be gone, but you can still talk to him whenever you want to." Her eyes went wide, angry again, shoving me away.

"He's not gone! He's coming back! He would never leave me!" She goes back to screaming, "I know he's not gone. You're both just pranking me. He's on vacation somewhere. That's where he's been! That's why he's been gone! Don't lie to me!"

She picked up the cutting board off the floor, washed it, and started chopping onions and other vegetables, with no method whatsoever.

"Be careful, you'll hurt yourself. Do you want me to do it instead?" I asked, hoping she'd put the knife down before she cut herself. I walked toward her slowly. "Honey, come relax for a few minutes." I grabbed her arm gently, trying to ease her out of whatever has come over her, like I did before. "Lilian. Lilian, I need you to talk to me." I eased my other hand around the wrist of the hand she held the knife with.

Her breathing started to slow until she realized what I was doing. Her pupils dilated, all hopes of cooperation lost. "Lilian, please, just calm down." I tightened my grip in case, but she was faster than me. She slipped out of my hold, and rushed around to the other side of the island countertop. "Lilian! Please, Lilian! We can work through this. You *will* be alright. I'll get you someone to talk to. We can even go together if you want. I love—"

But she charged at me, and everything went black as my head hit the counter and I fell to the ground.

When I woke up, I could float, and go through walls, and no one could see me. I don't blame her for what she did. She was hurt—something was going on. She couldn't help it. She wasn't herself. I don't think she ever will be again. I watch her now, and she doesn't seem happy, but she seems at peace. And I'm happy for her. She'll make it. Even if I didn't.

I Am Expecting To Be Noticed – Zary Fekete (they/them)

I like thinking that people notice me. Because I am expecting to be noticed I fancy that people's opinion of me is good. There are certain things I try to do as I anticipate being watched.

When I wheel my trash can out on Thursday evenings I always make sure that the can is neatly pushed up against the curb. When I walk back toward the apartment-building, I imagine that someone has seen this and is impressed with me. "He cares," they must think.

The bird sounds were becoming more and more difficult to ignore. The apartment-building I live in is old enough now for there to be the occasional loose fitting on the outer walls—one of these fittings had slipped, creating a hole large enough for a bird to use. A bird did use it and now there's a nest behind the bookshelf in the guest bedroom.

This is what it looks like to be an upper-middle class citizen. I can afford to live in an apartment building that is old enough to be considered quaint but which also has certain quirks. My friends from the suburbs rave about where I live. It makes me feel good, important. But in order to have envious friends, one needs to put up with life in an old building. This is the price one pays.

When I order my coffee every morning, I make it a point to establish eye contact with the coffee shop employees. I smile at them at all the right times. After stirring in my sugar, I fold the empty paper packets crisply and then I throw them in the appropriate, approved recycling container. I expect the baristas have noticed this. I wouldn't be surprised if when I enter the coffeeshop that each one of them might silently hope that they are given the chance to wait on me that day. They might even mention it to one another—like it's a playful game. I am different, and they've noticed.

The initial bird was not an issue because it was quiet. When the eggs hatched was when I realized I had a problem. When this building had been built in the late 19th century the rooms had ornate shelves built into the walls. It was part of the place's charm. Because of this I couldn't just pull the bookshelf away from the wall to potentially free the birds or move the nest or do any other unnamed thing so that I wouldn't need to hear the chirps throughout the day.

The chirping always began around dawn. Because I sleep with a fan on in the background, for white noise, I didn't notice the chirping until I woke up and turned off the fan. Then I would hear it, and the chirps felt like an itch that couldn't be scratched. Suddenly I would be thinking about this unseen and disagreeable nest which was just inches from my interior life. I felt dirty. Nature had found a way to distress the equilibrium I had amassed for myself.

When I fill up my car at the gas station I know that someone must be observing as I clean off my windshield. I pull the squeegee in crisp strokes with just the right amount of pressure against the glass. I form rivulets of water with each pull and the smooth streams that form on the metal impresses and soothes me. Only a very talented person with a true care for humanity could manage his life and handle his car like I do. This is the kind of person I am.

Finally, I called my neighbor because I know that he does a lot of handiwork around his apartment. He has seven children, and in half an hour he knocked on my door, toolbox in hand, with his two youngest kids standing behind him. He said that whenever he does any work he tries to make sure that some of his kids are around to watch, because any life experience is worth watching.

My neighbor took out a skill saw. He plugged it into an electrical outlet and then stood on a chair so that he could get a better view of the upper sections of the shelves. He tapped on the wood a few times, sort of like he was checking a melon for ripeness. He flicked the power switch on his saw and began to cut a slice of wood out of the upper shelf.

In about a minute he had an opening large enough so that he could peer behind the shelf unit. He was using a small flashlight. He said, yes, he could see the nest. He grabbed a hammer, reached through the hole in the shelf, and crushed the baby birds. When he pulled the hammer out it was covered with blood and feathers. This fascinated his kids. He then grabbed an old t-shirt and stuffed up the hole he had cut.

He told me to call him if the mother bird came back to build another nest. I didn't suppose she would.

I have friends coming to my place for dinner tonight. I have already anticipated what we might talk about and have mentally prepared several comments that are political, up to date and relevant. My guests will enjoy their time with me and feel glad to have been invited. I might even tell them about certain parts of the bird story. Certain parts.

NON-FICTION

"Let faith oust fact; let fancy oust memory; I look deep down and do believe." – Gina Twardosz (she/her)

It was summer, and when my mother and I were driving through the corn fields she hit a bird. It thumped across the hood then the windshield—or maybe the windshield then the hood—landing limp on the other side of the road. She stopped for a minute and turned on the wipers before starting again. There wasn't any blood, just dust. I think it might've been a blackbird or a magpie. I don't know if she remembers, but sometimes when I'm walking and I see several black birds hovering I think I should've done something then. But we drove on, leaving the outskirts until we reached something more civilized with streetlights and freshly paved black tar. We paused at a stoplight, waiting for the signal to go, hearing a distant honking that grew louder until it was surrounding us. "Oh," my mother said, "it's a funeral procession." A hearse drove through the red light.

"Why do they do that?"

"Do what, not stop?"

"Yeah."

"I don't know, I guess so they can all stay together. But it's like we're paying our respects, too." My mother honked her horn lightly. "You know, I want to be cremated when I die. And you can take half, and your brother can have the other half."

The last car pulled through the light and we drove on.

We were closer then, or at least, we could talk to each other in real conversation. Whenever I picture her, I see her in that beat up blue jeep, its dashboard spotted with warning lights. She's always driving somewhere, pushing the limits of automobile longevity. I walk mostly everywhere now, miles and miles as if something at my core grows in hunger when I'm stationary, satiated only when restless legs do their walking. I don't really sleep at night. The evening surprises me, its curtain of darkness falling, dropping with black sandbags; I don't like its permanence: a somewhat kinder suffocation. At night, I cannot rest. The synapses in my brain continue to fire off well into the night, each thought crackling to life, ricocheting off my skull like a bullet in a tin can. I shout in my sleep, incomprehensible utterings, the ferocity of which is more unsettling than the content. I used to sleepwalk. I'd open the bedroom door, make it down a flight of stairs and undo the latch on the back door. I was stopped, fortunately enough, by the second lock on the bottom of the sliding door. In my somnambulistic state, I always forgot this second lock. Who knows where I would have ended up. I didn't even know where I was trying to go at that time of night—I was just trying to leave.

Those nights when my body was in control seemed never ending. My mind was on autopilot, just trying to keep up with its determined insatiability to flee. There was an element of fear each morning when I wearily awoke and surveyed my seemingly unfamiliar surroundings. Some nights I'd awake on the couch, while other times I'd be on the floor, the rug just below my bed burning a ripe strawberry brand into my cheek. Both my father and my uncle feared I'd someday fall out a window for I was so completely at the mercy of my body that I would do whatever it wanted done without ever waking up.

My sleepwalking reached its height after my parents' divorce, when I was still adjusting to a new, motherless life. I missed the idea of her most of all; I missed having some kind of mother, even though she was, and always will be, it. In the mornings I leave my bed and move my body just to say that I can. I feel as though I am pursuing happiness like a hound pursues a fox through a thicket of sharp brush. I am at a loss for something.

Sometimes, when I'm on the road with Catholics and an ambulance passes, they'll pray. One friend holds her breath while passing a cemetery. In Chicago, all the cemeteries are long and I resist the urge to laugh when I see her face start to tinge ruby. When I drove, I used to pray all the time, mostly because I was bad at maneuvering the mechanical animal. I used to drink, too, although never while driving; I used to drive hungover, though, which is somehow worse. I still drink. Occasionally, I do drugs although I never ask for them. My mother never taught me how to drive so she used to white knuckle the handle on the car's door. I was never a bad driver, just constantly anxious at what the other drivers could possibly be thinking. I was always trying to predict the future, who would merge when, or where, or even why, why would they merge then, trapping me between two trucks? On highways, I'd have to pull over onto the shoulder and cry out. Once, I saw a sedan with the bumper sticker "Don't follow me, I don't know where I'm going!"

When my parents divorced, my father worked longer hours. At some point, I couldn't be both mother and father to myself, so I spent most of my time at my uncle's house. He didn't have a job, so he worked around the house while his wife worked at the hospital. He had time to spend with me, at least, whereas other people didn't. The babysitting was slow-going at first. On my first visit, I spent hours hunched under the table crying, having reached my limit of pseudo parents. His older dog, Mandy, eyed me suspiciously from where she lay over the floor's heating vent in intermittent slumber. That was the entirety of my childhood: hiding under the roundness of a shadow of dull wood. It was only after some time that my uncle could entice me out from under with a blizzard from Dairy Queen. Oreo was my favorite. We'd go on long walks in search of them because his wife drove the car to work. Ice cream tastes so good when you're tired or weak from walking.

My uncle lived in the last house at the end of a cul-de-sac flanked on either side by thick woods and sometimes we would go out wandering the trails besieged by thick brush. It was exhilarating to pick burrs out of my socks at the end of the night. We'd track tracks but turn back when the path got too muddy with spillover from the pond. In the winter, the pond would freeze over so solidly that boys from the neighborhood would play hockey, dotting the ice with rocks which were boundaries for goals. My uncle would watch the hockey players from the window with a sense of longing, the dull ache of his joints keeping him inside. I would sit with him, stifling my desire to learn how to skate or be seen.

When the ice melted, I'd return to the yard skipping stones across a sea of grass because I've never been to the sea, and my East Coast friends say that Lake Michigan is no substitute for the real thing. Daisy, my uncle's puppy, would trample patches into mud, chasing them as if they were treats. We'd play fetch until it grew dark, or until the stones drooled more than the dog's maw, and then we'd head inside.

One night I walked inside to find my uncle crying. I had never thought men capable of crying before. I found my father to be immovable, so it was startling to see my uncle's tears free flowing. He was holding a drawing in his hand, one I had done on lined paper about an hour before. At the center was a frenzied glob of black colored pencil strokes arranged somewhat sentimentally into the shape of a dog. Around the dog were the words "my best friend Daisy." I didn't think it was that bad of a drawing to elicit that sort of reaction.

"Jean, you have friends at school, right? What about those girls who came to your birthday party—you still see them, right?"

I saw Carissa, Jayde, and Karla every day at lunch. We were close, although not as close as the characters you'd find in a coming-of-age movie about female friendship. Still, my uncle cried.

When my father arrived, they talked for a few minutes without me. From the stairs where I sat lacing up my boots, I saw my uncle show my father the picture. My father waved his hands dismissively and called for me. During the car ride home, I asked what was so wrong.

"He thinks you don't have any friends," my father said, "like the dog is your only friend or something." I sat with this revelation for a minute.

"I have friends."

"You know he's sensitive. Everything bothers him, that's why he drinks. He was loaded now anyway, doesn't even know what he's saying."

"What do you mean?"

"I mean, he's drunk, Gina. He hides the bottle from his wife in the ceiling and drinks while she's at work and he's watching you." I could feel his annoyance as sharply as the wind coming from the open window, but I couldn't tell who it was directed at: me, my uncle, or himself for letting a man who drank watch his child. To me it made no difference that my uncle drank. It was simply new information, something I hadn't considered before. I would file that information away for many years, silently wondering what it all meant—that my uncle drank to be happy and that my grandfather had drunk himself into an early grave and that my militant father didn't drink at all. Eventually, I would outgrow the need for a babysitter and finally my uncle would sober up. I went to college and didn't start drinking until I turned 21. For a long time after that, I didn't stop.

It feels like you're always driving in Indiana as everything is spaced so far apart. If you don't have a car, it's as though you're stranded. Walking feels stigmatized and is occasionally impossible. My friend drove through the towns neighboring my hometown on her way to the Dunes and she said she had never felt more depressed. *How can people live like that?* She was thinking out loud about poverty, steel mills and chemical detritus. I had spent 18 years of my life living like that. It made me eager to leave.

My father's great grandmother was Polish and "straight off the boat" as some with less eloquence than I purport might say, and she never spoke a lick of English. Good for her, I think, but all her secrets died with her like the little candies she would give my father after he mowed her lawn or washed the car she didn't know how to drive. *Busha*, he said. "Busia" is grandmother. I do not know her real name.

There are many things I don't know, and I can't just sit there and let the uncertainty gnaw at my bones. I'm not roadkill. I seek the sprightly truth. My father and I used to watch a show called

Kolchak: The Night Stalker that was canceled after one season. A frumpy journalist prone to mishap, Carl Kolchak wanders Chicago proving the otherwise improvable: monsters are real. His camera always gets broken by the end of the episode, though, and only he knows the truth. Things like names and dates get lost in my family lore. My mother is also a pathological liar, so it is hard to trust the tales she tells about herself unless one keeps track of them with meticulous detail, comparing and contrasting different retellings in order to suss out some sort of truth. No; there is no such thing as "some sort of truth." Truth is whole, always with a capital T—anything less is a lie. I have to be careful. I must hold myself to certain standards as the truth keeper.

the title of this piece is a quote taken from Herman Melville's Moby Dick

Laughing, Before the Wreck – Gina Twardosz (she/her)

My father always asks me when I'm going to help him write his memoir, and some days I consider buying him one of those dictation machines and just letting him go until it spins out. I think it would be at first terrible, then revered, like how things that were once obscure garbage often are when society changes. I read about a comic book artist who drew graphic depictions of violence against women; people were rightly appalled, and if he hadn't been a recluse, they would've called for his imprisonment. But some have argued that he was doing exactly what he was supposed to: channeling the darkness into art and not onto women.

My father embellishes his stories, as we all do; our fixations are our bluffs or tells. We are a family who loves a good story—even the ghastly ones—and those stories get repeated over and over, passed down like family lore. My father and my uncle love telling stories about their hometown's family doctor who was run out of town when he didn't catch an elderly woman's cancer in time and she died; this broke him and he turned to pills. He also became a hoarder, and my father and uncle would make monthly visits to his home, attempting to help free the man of his clutter and occasionally pocket the loose change and dollar bills they'd find lying around. Once, they stumbled across his VHS porn stash and were surprised to learn that many of the young women were dressed as little girls and I hate these stories because once, when I was a little girl, I went to him for a check-up when he was still in practice and I have trouble not looking back on that moment with a colored lens.

He died in that hoarder's house of a drug overdose, penniless and alone.

I do not enjoy telling bad stories and yet they persist. I think that, at any moment, I can just start writing fiction and free myself from the confines of the truth. I could say that he was a good doctor who cured millions and delivered babies on buses and trains. I think that I could write anything and you'd all believe it. It's too great of power to wield, however: spending all my time trying to convince you of a lie is really quite exhausting. I'd much rather record real life—life does all my work for me. I think I'm incapable of really lying, or I'm a bad bluffer because you can read my face instantly. We're all lying, really, so much and so often.

I wonder what my father would have me write about—that he was once an artist, but couldn't afford art school or had to work at his father's gas station all throughout his teens and was worried he'd get his neck wrung when they ran out of gas during the gas shortage or get shot and robbed, robbed then shot?

We spent a lonesome Covid-19 winter together once after I got several impacted wisdom teeth removed. I was bleeding so much, propped up on the couch because if I slept lying down I would have probably choked on all the blood soaked gauze. My father dug through our DVDs, searching for a way to distract me from my pain. This was not entirely out of the ordinary, however; we've always watched movies together, since I was little. My father knows everything about movies like facts and trivia or actors' names and ages. He is impossible to watch a new movie with because of his constant chattering, but he's a good companion when you're watching a movie you've seen before, like *Jaws*, which would have been somewhat ironic considering my condition, but it was both our favorite movie. Spurred by my father, I've learned a lot about the movie over the years. I've listened to podcasts and read books and essays. I appreciate its humor—thanks to little known improviser Carl Gottlieb—yet its honest portrayal of the evils of a capitalistic society. It's full of allegories, practically a book inside a book—a movie inside a movie based on real life events. My father and I enjoy the comedic bickering of Hooper and Quint, which was nearly real as both the actors really disliked one another.

"You have city hands, Mr. Hooper," Quint says to the young scientist.

"Hey, I don't need this...I don't need this working-class-hero crap!"

I've read essays that approach *Juws* through a feminist lens, somewhat satirically since the movie's cast happens to be mostly male, but some astutely look at the shark as a sort of *vagina dentata* that reaps its revenge on the crusty, misogynistic sailor Quint. I wonder about this fascination I have with the stories of men. I've read *Moby Dick* again and again, but there's only two female characters in the entire sprawling book and they are mostly the butt of a bad joke. "I widowed that poor girl when I married her," says Captain Ahab about his wife. Chief Brody, as well, almost widows his wife as he sets off, somewhat short-sightedly, to kill the behemoth shark.

Yet, I have always idolized the character of Chief Brody, a man with a will but not a way out, whose one job is to protect the people of Amity yet is down and out before he even starts. Brody is decidedly a traditionally masculine character but he is not without fear. He's scared of the water and he's scared for the lives of the people in the town, including his family. In the end, it is Brody who kills the shark. Not Quint, whose violent machismo and inability to see the big picture is his ultimate undoing, eaten and sunken by his obsession;

nor is it Hooper, who, with all the technological advances available to him, runs and hides, almost mucking everything up with the futility of his plan. It is Brody, a true middleman, who defeats the evil that has plagued the seaside town for much too long.

My father seemed to idolize Chief Brody, too, but for different reasons. His favorite part was the hunt for the beast—three men at their most macho with nothing between them and the monster but an abyss that often stared right back into their souls. I preferred the beginning exposition, when the characters of the hermetically sealed world of the town seem to come alive in their self-centeredness and short sightedness.

"That's all pointless," my father would say. "The real focus of the movie is when they're out on the boat. That's when it gets good."

It's curious that my father would favor a lawman, as increasingly when he reflects back upon his life he sees himself as a persecuted outlaw. Married thrice and forced to work since the age of fourteen, he paints a romantic picture of his struggle. I knew once the movie ended he would launch into a soliloquy—he couldn't go more than three hours without hearing the sound of his own voice.

"I've never met a sheriff like Chief Brody."

I knew this story well, but I still let him tell it anyway, because when he did, I could see that he was there reliving it. I knew my father through the stories he told, and while there were many plot holes and frayed ends, the tapestry he wove told me more about his life than any actual event. In the movie of my father's life he was a cowboy on the run from everything and everyone. This imagined self helped him justify his mistakes, and this felt like something only

I could understand, so I let him be his own protagonist for a little while.

It was the cut of the wind as he raced past a bygone era of long blond hair—past decades of cigarettes and late nights and a home which moved almost as quickly as his frantic thoughts—that was the most memorable. It was a moment of freedom; he, still a young man at this point, cut loose like a buck, still reeling from the tremble of a rifle blast through mid-air after a situation that felt impossibly constraining.

This was the moment he'd always remember.

"Not many people can say they outran the cops," he said to me with a smirk on his face. He didn't drink anymore, but if he did, he'd retell this roadrunner tale with a glass of blackberry brandy in his hand. My father's favorite song was Elton John's "Elderberry Wine" and I always confused the two, blackberry brandy and elderberry wine.

This was during his divorce from his second wife. He had come to the trailer for a box of his things, mostly collectible knives and magazines. He couldn't take the fish tank full of tropical fish and he would regret this for most of his life. He sat on the picnic table in the lot that was supposed to be their yard and made a meticulous list of all the things that were his—almost thirty years later, he would still craft a makeshift list before going out anywhere.

"Those dicks called the cops on me because they always sided with her," he said of his neighbors. If this were the Wild West, my father was the outlaw, Kid Rock's "Cowboy," and his neighbor, a drug dealing guitar player who kept half the park up at night with his insufferable twanging, was the deputy. The real sheriffs were only a phone call away. Ballsy is the drug dealer who associates with cops, but my father was never one to leave a good impression on anyone.

His wife had filed a petty restraining order against him and, by going to collect his meager belongings, he was in violation. When the cops arrived, my father was on the picnic table. He was a thin man, who spoke concisely and probably didn't pose much of a threat to the officers. But, my father was also a dirty blond with a skull tattoo on his wrist and a Mickey Mouse tattoo on his calf. He reeked of menthol, a fragrance of concentrated anxiety, so he probably set off some red flags. The cops were defensive, yet my father was on the offense.

"Can you shoot me?" he called out to the officers.

"No, we can't shoot you," one of them said, "but, we have to cuff you." That's when my father started to run.

Dropping his things and leaping off the picnic table, he streaked through the trailer park, tailed by the officers who were only a few steps behind him. He caught a second wind on the outskirts of the park with a chain link fence in sight. The fence was daunting. It was singed with rust and twelve feet high but my father, adrenaline coursing through his veins and on the cusp of freedom, didn't stop to think about what lay in his way. He hopped the chainmail fence, all twelve feet of it, and the cops returned to their black and whites, calling in a warrant for my father who was always just a little too fast, both in making decisions and mistakes. They couldn't pursue him because he had hopped the fence into an entirely different state. He had fled the police across the Indiana/Illinois border, and as Illinois begrudgingly accepted my father—and not for the last time—the police realized that they had lost jurisdiction.

He wouldn't outsmart the cops, of course. They would haul him in hours later, having marked him as he returned to the bank for which he did outdoor maintenance work. But he would outrun them, and that, in itself, was victory enough.

"Tat muhst've sucked," I said, breaking the flow of the story with the mushiness of my wounded sputtering.

"Pfft. Bitch sold my fish after that, too."

"Didya ever misser?"

"Not after that shit she pulled, no," and then, after a long pause, "I don't know if I ever loved her. I guess it doesn't really matter now."

On the Pulse of a Neighborhood :: No Pruning Required – Jen Schneider (she/her)

i could parse the etymology of its naming. *spring garden*—in nondescript terms. carefully curated, then dissected and carved. spring, as a verb, *to burst, sprout, flow forth*. and a noun - *tide, branch. a kind of dance*. with clippings (no longer in newspaper print) of *day-springs, springtime, and spring tides*. high and low. adjectives unknown. and garden—nouns of *orchards and palace grounds*. with goals *to grasp*, then *enclose*. a descriptor for *parties, varieties, paths, and glass*. residents deemed scrappy. skies often scraping. building structures mostly made of brick and mortar. windowpanes and bird migrations often breaking. hands kneed play doh. knuckles crack apples and sidewalk asphalt. shards gather on brick front porch stoops. in pails and plastic cups. ice scooped. companions and compadres consume swirls of soft serve and sliced steak. seasonings of pepper and onion appropriately diced. food truck wheels require (t)oil. soil both breathes and consumes life. equally action oriented. to lay out. to cultivate. of hand. by trowel. with hoe. forms of both speech and states of being. pruners and pruning. nouns and verbs. forms of speech and states of being. in an ongoing tug of war. tenses and tensions on all corners. the scent (and secrets) of place and peanuts roasting. honey simultaneously thick and trapping. origins, mostly unknown. both spring and garden, grounded (if not united) in life. layered of longing. flavored of cherry suckers, salted pretzels, and sour apples. ready to be picked. not plucked. hoping for some neighborly luck. while propositions and prepositions tango. then waltz. through and of backyard freezers, curbside refrigerator cubes, and rotating doors. fingerprint smudges. shoulder grudges. souls in rubber soles pound soil, then concrete. lights red, green, and yellow blink. carefree cautions. curious blends (coffee roasters a popular purveyor) of stop and go. cultivated terraced set ups. generational seeds. spuds and sprouts. varying degrees of clout. new life forms. formation a blend both functional and happenstance. a destination for business magnates (first) and biodiversity (second). in *a major* and community college life forms. potential clothed in high-rise denim and low-top converse most mondays. lycra and layers on tuesday. puffers (and puffins) come winter. tanks (and tankers) come may. the army-navy game as regular as the no. 2 line. simultaneously divine. i could parse the etymology of its naming. *spring garden*. but i don't. it's easy to see. visions (non-fiction) and plots (land) united in growth and reimagined forms. on soils rich in ABCs and 123s. square portfolios (faux leather). eight and a half by eleven spirals. composition notebooks and ceramics. acronym soup - A&P, student IDs. mints (money and lifesavers) and mayhem (systems often slow). logarithms and computer log-ins. learning and leaning a common thread. 100% original. combat books (doc martin and doc aspirants). biology on wednesdays and thursdays. english 101 a hybrid. the trolley (re)tired. history required in semester 2. developments on all corners. telescopes to the stars. binoculars and magnified glasses. a small garden. a blend of cranberry red and boysenberry hues. squared. perimeters of chain fences. string lights twinkle. as orion and beetlejuice mingle. seeds are planted. water is applied. No. 2s scratch new soil. a neighborhood just north of __ and just south of __. east and west of somewhere, too. everyone's tile. also, someone's origins. a place called home. all doors clocked. signs of the times. shopping at all hours. in library stacks and big box stocks. cars and mini marts. on corners. under bridges. springs and gardens. always flowing. along with the pulse (trains beneath feet, pigeons on electric wires) of the neighborhood. most minding red Ps and green Fs. neither vitamin dense nor envious. sustenance and smiles shaded by shadows. of tattletale gray. the yellow sun peaks. then plays hide and go seek. curiosity always pressing. the pulse of a spring garden. nestled in the winding ropes and limbs of the nearby park. and the parkway. of trolleys and trains. boat houses and books. approaching hill sides with more soil. more firsts (zoos, signing, sightings). and thirst. for history yet threaded. hues of harmony. fabrics (cotton, wool, tweed, plaid) long eroded. then reimagined. molten. of one. with soil and story. of the neighborhood. and the community. in spring garden. i could parse the etymology of its naming. but i don't. meaning a blend of living and paths yet to be sown. pruning not needed. present pulses perfectly conspired. much more than a garden of grammar and gravitas. Much more than a spring of historical song. a genre appropriately inspired. cultivated in style. a lot of many (p)lots. ready to be told.

Haunted by the Women Before Us – Nicole Garner (she/her)

I've found, time and again, that there are connections that resonate through space and time between people who have had similar experiences, and if we look in the right places, we can find others who speak to us of things only they can understand. Our stories come together, meeting on the edges of when and where, in spaces that only exist for those of us who have lived our entire lives being taught that there is something wrong with women who love each other. I think that, just maybe, our stories stay in those spaces, unheard, even though there are so many others who need them, too.

When my partner died, I found myself in one of those spaces, and I found the stories that were waiting for me. I've found repetitions of the experiences of lesbian relationships that stretch from ancient Sumeria until today. My partner wasn't fortunate enough to hear these stories when she was alive, so now, I write them again, in letters to her, to all of the others like us who have no one where they are who will tell them that there can never be anything wrong with loving someone, that in fact, love is the one thing that is always right. This lets me honor our history while, at the same time, I am also compiling a history of the women who came before us, in a way in which this hasn't been done before, telling the stories experience by experience, through the repetitions that echo to us through time and space.

Many of the women writers who have influenced me, such as Natalie Barney, Djuna Barnes, Sylvia Beach, and Janet Flanner had chosen to emigrate to Paris during the Belle Epoque because they could be free in Paris in ways that they could not be in the United States. Once they were living in Paris they joined with many other women like them, some, like Colette and Liane de Poughy, who were from France, others like Radclyffe Hall and Renee Vivien, who were from England. These women made new ways of being and living, they created new art forms, reclaimed historical figures and myths, created new forms of literature, and made entirely new cultures in which they, and others like them, could be who they were without collapsing into the kind of assimilation that we see so often. These women laid the foundation for new ways of living that we can pick up the threads of even now.

All these women who were working in Paris at that time have enriched my life greatly; they have given me a history, a culture, and a blueprint for life. The woman from that time who has had the greatest impact on me is Natalie Barney. Natalie not only made a space in which others could learn to feel safe and to accept themselves so that they could grow, but she also wrote about her separation from Renee Vivien, and later, Renee's death.

This is some of my work, from one of my letters, my attempt to add to the culture that has been passed down, from woman to woman, to carry on the tradition of forming new traditions:

Sometimes I think about how many of us have been separated, only for one to later die, and how few times our stories have been told! Imagine how different things could be for other women who could read what I'm writing to you and maybe they could find out in time, before anyone else dies of hate. The more I learn about these women the more I need to tell you about them, about how they lived and the things that they did, about how they loved. Our love story is a part of their love stories, too. I think that if I put all of that love together that there will be a change, at least for us, even if you aren't here. I know, too, that there are other women like us, now, who need to know about all of these loves so that, just maybe, they can have happier endings. Too many stories like ours have gone untold and you deserve more than that. Most of all I need to tell you these stories of us and of them and of me, without you. I know that I can't send you these letters, but I want all of this love to rise to you, like a prayer, so that wherever you are you can feel it.

I don't know how it felt for you when you died, but I do know that when I heard those words it felt like I was dying, too, and I hoped that I was. It felt like all of the oxygen just caught fire, like even molecules couldn't bear to exist without you. Every cell in my body burned like that for the longest time, I couldn't breathe, couldn't get enough oxygen for months. It still happens almost every day, out of the blue, anything, a song, the sky, that shade of pink that you loved, anything, nothing, and all of a sudden the air that I'm breathing is fire and no one else knows. I know, at those times, that what I am feeling is *the lack* of you. The world is so heavy without you. Sometimes I panic because there is nothing that anyone can ever do to make this stop. Sometimes, when I see couples, like we were, young women, even though my heart dances to see them able to be out, it hurts, so much, and I think about how amazing it was to have someone to share everything with. Sometimes when I see couples, like we were supposed to be, older women, it's like I lose you again, before we even were supposed to be them. How much history could we have had between us?

I used to try to find books about grief, about losing someone; I thought that they would help. They didn't, you know, they were all about women and men and that is not at all the same thing. The only person I have ever read who can make me feel like she knows what I feel is Natalie Barney. Remember, I was telling you about her?

Natalie is so important to me for so very many reasons, but one of the most important is that I had started reading her the day before I found out that you had died! Anyway, for a few days I couldn't read or do anything because every time that I started to do anything I would think how could she be dead? And then everything else would be gone in that fire I was breathing. So, on my birthday, I went to a café with my book of Natalie's writings and I sat outside, soaking in the sun, you know, like you always did—I was, I'm sure, trying to soak you in. I had known that Natalie and Renee had been together for a long time and that their families had split them up. I knew that Renee died, about two years later, so I went right to the piece that she had written about Renee shortly after she died. She wasn't there either, when Renee died, she, too, wasn't allowed to be. She got there right after; Renee must have died while she was walking there because the butler told her that Renee had just died. What she said next makes me pretty sure that she also knows what it feels like to have all of the air catch on fire: "I staggered away, back to the Avenue du Bois, and fainted on the nearest bench. When I regained consciousness, I went home and shut myself up in my bedroom. Unable and unwilling to see her dead, I needed to get into contact immediately with all that I had left of her. Like a grave robber I fell upon the precious casket she had given me. The key was lost and I had to force the lock. It held so many tangible memories that I felt her presence around me. No one could stop her from joining me now. May I be forever haunted! For if the haunting stopped, what would be left? Oblivion." That is exactly how I felt! I know that she fainted from the way that the air catches fire when the woman that we have loved more than ourselves has died alone and we have not been permitted to tell her that we love her one more time. She even knows that the only way that she could have had Renee is for her to haunt her after she had died because, if they were both alive, no one would let them be together. When I read that I thought oh! Really! That is it! I, too, hoped to be haunted. She also wanted to try to bring Renee back, through her writing and through her life.

Her grief is affected by the enforced separation and by the kind of relationship they had before their families discovered their love. Unlike people who can openly be together, Natalie and Renee had to hide their love and to live in fear of being found out. While Natalie had a sense of herself that allowed her to believe that, no matter what others said, there is never anything wrong with love, Renee was not in a place from which she could believe that, and much of their relationship had been taken up with—just like ours— her guilt and shame about their love. You know what else, if I am telling you every little thing like always? Renee was a lot like you, and she thought about dying and death much of the time. We can talk about that, later, though. Well maybe this now: Natalie thought that each of them were responding to their separation and the hate in their families courageously. She said, "Courage after love: She dared to die...I dared to live."

ABOUT THE CONTRIBUTORS

- A. Bhardwaj (she/her) writes and reads whenever she can. She loves drawing inspiration from the world around her and her daily experiences.

- Abigail Kangas is a high school senior living in Virginia. This is her first publication, but she has been writing short stories and poetry since she was thirteen years old. She is pursuing an education and career in forensic science, starting with the program at Virginia Commonwealth University. She hopes to continue writing throughout her life, even if only for fun.

- Alexandria is a Georgia native and attended the University of Georgia, earning a B.A. in International Affairs and a Master's in Public Administration. Since, she has spent significant time abroad studying community development and working alongside government officials and non-profit organizations to obtain AIDS relief funding for underserved and often disregarded populations in Africa, the Caribbean, and Central and South America. In her free time from her career in public health, she enjoys writing, biking, painting, collecting art, and traveling.

- Alice Louise Lannon is Scottish poet and writer of creative non-fiction. She holds an MLitt in Creative Writing from The University of Glasgow. Her publication credits include *Wet Grain* and *From Glasgow to Saturn.* She is also the editor of *heather,* an anthology of new Scottish writing and art, which was released in June 2022. Currently she is working on a book about the sea & storytelling & women's narratives, for which she has received funding from Arts Go Global.

- Allison Fradkin (she/her) delights in applying her Women's & Gender Studies education to the creation of satirically scintillating poems, prose, and plays that (sur)pass the Bechdel Test and enlist their characters in a caricature of the idiocies and intricacies of insidious isms. An enthusiast of inclusivity and accessibility, Fradkin freelances for her hometown of Chicago as Literary Manager of Violet Surprise Theatre, curating new works by queer playwrights; Co-Artistic Director of Mosaic Players, presenting historical plays that champion social justice; and Dramatist for Special Gifts Theatre, adapting scripts for actors of all abilities. Allison's auxiliary activities include vintage shopping, volunteering, and tending to her thespian tendencies.

- Ann Kammerer lives in Oak Park, Illinois, where she is a semi-retired copy and feature writer for small business and higher education. Her short fiction and poetry have appeared in several regional publications, magazines and on-line platforms, including *The Thoughtful Dog, Open Arts Forum,* and *The*

Ekphrastic Review. She received top honors in fiction writing contests run by the Chicago-based Crow Woods Publishing and Toledo/Ann Arbor's *Current Magazine*, and she made the top 10 in the 2018 Tillie Olsen Short Fiction Award sponsored by *The Tishman Review.* Ann's fiction was featured in the 2015 and 2020 anthologies of art-inspired short stories, *Visions of Life* and *Visions of Life 2,* produced by Crow Woods Publishing.

❖ Anna Emilia was born in Newark, NJ to a Black and Japanese Entrepreneurial Mother and Indo-Trinidadian Immigrant father. She has received her Bachelor's in business Administration from Berkeley College and since then obtained her CPR/BLS, Life Coach and Reiki certifications. When she has free time, it is usually spent drinking coffee, writing more poetry, watching Bob's Burgers, playing with her Shihtzu Chewy or relaxing in nature! She has been published in *Dreams in Hiding Anthology, Prosetics,* and others! She is also working on her first chapbook! Instagram @annaemiliapoetry

❖ Aya Sunga Askert is a multidisciplinary artist who writes poetry and creates three dimensional objects such as assemblages, sculptures, and installations. Born and bred in the Philippines, Aya's passion in shaping, building, and assembling objects (and sentences) together is deeply rooted since childhood. As early as the age of 6, she started making her own toys out of found objects and materials from nature. Aya started to write during her teenage years where she penned down politically charged poems and essays for her high school paper. Nowadays, she writes about love, self-healing, and nature. Before becoming a full-time artist, Aya worked as a professional fashion model for 6 years in Asia, then as an early childhood educator for 16 years in Sweden. She advocated the Reggio Emelia pedagogy, an educational philosophy that believes that every child is creative, and learning is attained through exploration of the creative expressions such as writing, painting, music, and drama. IG @aya.infinityart

❖ Cassandra Traina (she/her/hers) is a recent graduate of Sarah Lawrence College. She lives in New York and France. Publications include *Love & Squalor, The Croaker, orangepeel Magazine, Action, Spectacle*, and *Healthline Magazine*. In 2020 she received an honorable mention from The Academy of American Poets College Prize for her poem NOV 26 // THANKSGIVING MORNING. In July and December 2022, she was an artist-in-residence at Chateau Orquevaux. In September 2022 she was a writer-in-residence at Cuttyhunk Island Writers' Residency, in workshop with award-winning poet Chen Chen. Currently, she is living and working with the administrative team at Chateau Orquevaux in Orquevaux, France. These poems are from her recently completed, unpublished poetry collection which takes the form of a poetic diary. Written from March 13, 2020 to March 21, 2021, each poem is dated as well as titled.

❖ Chris Dorian may not consider himself a poet at times, but once in a while he throws words out haphazardly that form somewhat cohesive compositions some may call poetry. He is from New Jersey, and you can find more of his work on FB/IG @CDorianPoetry

❖ Dani De Luca is a teacher and writer. She holds a BA in Portuguese Language and an MA in TESOL She resides outside Nashville with her husband and son.

❖ Dani Solace (they/he/she) is a Queer author, illustrator, and poet. She currently resides and works in Oklahoma City. More of his works can be found in their first collection of poetry, *A few moments of honesty*, and at <u>poetrybysolace.com</u>.

❖ Daniel Moreschi is a poet from Neath, South Wales, UK. After life was turned upside down by his ongoing battle with severe M.E., he rediscovered his passion for poetry that had been dormant since his teenage years. Writing has served as a distraction from his struggles ever since. Daniel has been acclaimed by many poetry competitions, including the annual ones hosted by the Oliver Goldsmith Literature Festival, Wine Country Writers Festival, Short Stories Unlimited, Michigan Poetry Society, Westmoreland Arts & Heritage Festival, Ohio Poetry Day, and Inchicore Ledwidge Society. Daniel has also had poetry published by The Society of Classical Poets, and The Black Cat Poetry Press

❖ Daniella Navarro is a part-time poet and full-time Hispanic American. She lives in Austin, TX, with Esmeralda, Juan Pablo, and Shane—two of whom are her cats, one of whom is her human boyfriend, but all of whom are house-trained. She started writing poems in the seventh grade and graduated from Texas State University with a bachelor's degree in creative writing. She works as an editor to provide a good life for her cats, but she hopes the five-day workweek is abolished once AI inevitably takes over.

❖ Danila Botha is the critically acclaimed author of short story collections *Got No Secrets* and the Trillium Book Award, Vine Awards, and ReLit Awards finalist *For All the Men (and Some of the Women I've Known)*. Her award-winning novel, *Too Much on the Inside* was published in 2015. She is currently working on her new graphic novel, and has a new collection of short stories, and a new novel coming out soon.

❖ Daphne Louber (she/her) is a writer, artist, and microbiologist based out of West Lafayette, Indiana. She loves interrogating the weird truths of the world and everything they touch. Her work is upcoming in the *Garfield Lake Review*, *The Last Girl Magazine*, and *Diet Milk Magazine*. She can be found on Instagram at @daphne.writes.

❖ Deron Eckert is a writer and attorney who lives in Lexington, Kentucky. His writing has appeared in *Rattle Magazine*, *Fahmidan Journal*, *Sky Island Journal*, *Swim Press*, *Treehouse Literary*, and *Rue Scribe* and is forthcoming in *Ghost City Review*. He is currently seeking representation for his Southern Gothic, coming-of-age novel, which explores how personal experiences change our preconceived notions of right and wrong.

❖ Dillon Charli is a queer author, dancer, and drag king from the unceded islands of Hawai'i, currently living on the occupied land of the Akimel O'odham tribe, otherwise known as Phoenix, Arizona. They began writing poetry at age 14 as a way to make sense of the challenges of living in poverty. They quickly discovered how powerful words can be to connect to your community, and published their first poem, *Twelve Little Birds*, in the University of Hilo's Art and Literary Magazine, *Kanilehua*, 2014-2015 edition. In 2018, Dillon self-published a collection of poetry on amazon, *Rigmarole of Reality*, dedicated to their grandma, who has always supported their writing. Since then, Dillon has written on and off while they pursue their graduate degree in social work but is hoping to get back in touch with their passion for writing, and the community writing creates.

❖ Elizabeth (Liz) Core Shenk (she/her) is a writer, yoga instructor, and mother based in northern Indiana. Elizabeth has published works in Swim Press's Issue 3: Sleep and [inherpspacejournal]'s Issue 1: Cake and Icing. Her debut chapbook Language of Flowers, explores the often complicated relationship between mothers and daughters, and the freedom that comes with releasing societal expectations of motherhood. In her spare time, you can find Elizabeth experimenting in the kitchen, reading historical fiction, or tromping through the woods near her home. To read more of her writing, you can find her on Instagram at @openwindowpoems.

❖ Elizabeth Motes (she/her) is a short story author and aspiring novelist. Her work has previously appeared in the *Trinity Review*, the *Outrageous Fortune* magazine, and in the *Venus Rising* anthology. She runs a writing account on Instagram (@emotes.writes) where she shares updates on her projects and writing tips.

❖ Emilija Veljković (she/her) is an amateur writer from Belgrade (Serbia). She writes poems and short stories, some of which have been published in *Sweetycat Press, redrosethorns magazine, Poetic Reveries*, etc. She's a lover of anime, and anything supernatural related.

❖ Emma Conally-Barklem (she/her) is a yogi, writer and poet based in Yorkshire, England. Pushcart Prize nominated, she was recently named as a New Northern Poet by Ilkley Poetry Festival and she had a summer residency at the Bronte Parsonage Museum. Her debut chapbook 'The Ridings' will be published by *Bent Key Publishing* in 2023 and her yoga & grief memoir, 'You Can't Hug a Butterfly: Love, Loss & Yoga' will be published by *QuillKeepers Press* in 2024.

❖ Ensol Baek (she/her) was born in Seoul, South Korea, grew up living in Seoul and Jeju, and now lives in the UK. She is currently a full-time student working on her undergraduate degree in English. Her poetic translations of the works of Baek Seok have appeared in *Polyglossia*, and more of her poetry can be found on her Instagram (@_tl_rks).

- ❖ Evan Violets is a lofi-loving soul who strings his dreams and thoughts into more literary expressions. His more specific passion lies in stringing together fragments of imagery to assemble a scene in audience minds. Whilst adventurous at experimenting with literary concepts, he isn't the best at experimenting in chemistry.

- ❖ Poussin teaches French and English at a university in Georgia, USA. His work in poetry and photography has appeared in Kestrel, Symposium, The Chimes, and many other publications worldwide. Most recently, his collections "In Absentia," and "If I Had a Gun," were published in 2021 and 2022 by *Silver Bow Publishing*.

- ❖ Fritz Dries (he/him) is just a guy. He has previously published two collections, Bury Your Teeth in the Yard and Four Seconds. Follow him on Twitter at @howlingmouth

- ❖ Gina Twardosz is a humorist and essayist from Chicago, IL. She primarily writes nonfiction but has experimented with short form essays and prose poetry. Her work has been featured in *Thimble Literary Magazine, Allium, A Journal of Poetry and Prose*, and Gotham's *The Razor*.

- ❖ Isabel de Silva is a 21-year-old poet from North Wales. She is currently studying a Master's degree in Celtic Studies. In her spare time she enjoys going for walks,complaining about being too hot (temperature-wise), and listening to Dungeons and Dragons podcasts. She can be found on Instagram at @idspoetry.

- ❖ Jacob "Jake" Teran is a proud Chicano living in the San Gabriel Valley, Los Angeles. Jake is a 2nd generation Chicano who was born in Montebello, Los Angeles, east of Los Angeles. He has published his first two short stories on Somos en Escrito, called "A Quiet Night on the Boulevard," "Niños del Sol," one short fictional story at his community college at Rio Hondo College, and a master's thesis for his graduate program, where he obtained his M.A. degree in Rhetoric and Composition. He is currently teaching composition to several departments in two colleges that include indigenous and Chicanx literature. In addition, Jake is an advocate for social justice, self-care, and embracing the identity of others. Jake is currently working on a novel based on his experiences growing up in his barrio that deals with gang lifestyle, drugs, violence, and finding one's Identity in a chaotic concrete jungle that he calls home.

- ❖ Jen Schneider is a community college educator who lives, works, and writes in small spaces throughout Pennsylvania.

- ❖ Jillian Calahan (she/her/they) is a poet and short story writer from Seattle, Washington. When she's not writing you can find her in a bookstore, chilling with her 4 cats and 2 dogs, crafting, or taking too many pictures of pretty sunsets. You can find her work on Instagram @novamarie_poetry

* K. L. Green is a bisexual poet and stage manager from San Jose, CA. She holds a BFA from the Boston University School of Theater and cares deeply about the importance of storytelling in all its forms. She started writing at a young age to help find sense in an often incoherent world. As she is frequently travelling for work on shows, she explores her place in constantly changing environments and relationships through poetry.

* K Weber (she/her) is an Ohio poet. She has self-published 7 free online book projects in PDF and audio formats. K has collaborated with over 200 people in her donated words poems; most of these can be found in her 3 most recent collections. Learn more, find her writing and photography credits, and access her e-chapbooks and audiobooks at kweberandherwords.com. You can also find her on Twitter & Instagram by username: midwesternskirt

* Kanishka Kataria (She/Her) is a girl of vision and power. She possesses the immense strength to transform the world with her articulation. Grown and brought up in New Delhi, India, she stays loyal to the values transferred to her by her parents. She is a writer and orator who strives to drive the world toward exhilaration and liberty through her articulation. She is recognized by more than 20 organizations for her work in literature, social issues, and scientific research. She believes in bringing the best of herself in every situation and holds faith in the universe to render back the vibrations of concern and appreciation.

* Karen Arredondo (she/they) is a Queer Mexican American writer and multidisciplinary artist working in San Antonio, Texas. Her first book of poetry Rose Gold will be out later this year. Karen has been published in several literary magazines and journals. Currently she is working on a series of short plays. Karen is an active member of the Blah Blah Blah poetry Spot as well as the Public Theater of San Antonio's Writer's Gym. Work can be found on her Instagram page @citaface3 or her website: www.karredondodesigns.com

* Karen E Fraser (she/her) is a Melbourne-based, published writer and poet. With degrees in Professional and Creative Writing, and Anthropology, Karen has held professional roles as a writer and editor. Her poetry embraces the beauty of the natural world; activism, advocacy and social justice; and the absolute necessity of freedom, love, dignity and belonging. Instagram: @be_nourished

* Of Maltese origin (b. 1982) Karina currently lives in France. She obtained a BA in Geography (Uni of Malta), a MSc in Sustainable Development (Imperial College and SOAS) and currently reading for a BA in English (Major) and Philosophy (Uni of London - Goldsmiths and Birkbeck). Her writing is made up of scraps of fragments, teasing rhythms and subtle colours. Some of her latest works include: *Soil dermis* – Ecotone, Cappadocia Journal of Environmental Humanities, 2022; *The Calling* – PEN Malta / PEN International, 2021; *Nights* – About Larkin, Journal of the Philip

Larkin Society UK, 2021; *Samsa unfurled* – Scintillas - A New Maltese Writing Anthology, 2021; *La Moselle* – a 2020 editor's choice is published in Survival Anthology by Hammond House Publishing UK, 2021; *The Geology of Baden-Württemberg*, *A Simple Matter of Conviction* and *Pleasure ground* – Les Cahiers Luxembourgeois, 2020. Presently she is working on her first poetry collection.

❖   Katherine E Winnick is a Japanese short form poet and member of the British Haiku Society, with work published in various journals, magazines, ezines and anthologies. Her poems can also be heard on the Haiku Pea Podcast and The Haiku Pond. Katherine is based in Brighton UK and works for Fabrica Art Gallery.

❖   Ken Anderson was a finalist in the 2021 Saints and Sinners poetry contest. *New Poetry from the Festival* (an anthology of the 2021/2022 winners and finalists) includes four of his poems. His poetry books are *The Intense Lover* and *Permanent Gardens*. Publications include *Angel Rust, Beyond Queer Words, Flux (Fifth Wheel Press), Gay and Lesbian Review, The Heart of Pride (Quillkeepers Press), Mollyhouse, Otherworlds Vol. 4 (Warning Lines), Prismatica, Queerlings, Rabid Oak, RFD, Screen Door, Vagabonds: Anthology of the Mad, Wicked Gay Ways,* and *Wussy Mag.*

❖   Kenneth Stephens is originally from India. He came to the United States to go to seminary and ended up with a PHD in philosophy. He has published a novel, Blaze Pascal and the Courage of Being (Adelaide Books), and a memoir, The Meaning of These Days: Memoir of a Philosophical Pastor (Wipf and Stock). He lives in Los Angeles County in a retirement community.

❖   Keon is a poet and visual artist currently based in Manchester, United Kingdom. His work challenges preconceptions and invents alternate worldviews. His most recent work can be seen in Kamena Magazine from the Warwick Writing Society. You can find his work on Instagram @keon_wong

❖   Laura Beth Johnson (she/her) is an award winning poet and songwriter based in Upstate New York known for her dark blend of story and soul. She was awarded the Lucy Monro Brooker Poetry Prize from the University of Indianapolis in 2017. In 2019, Laura was awarded a Songwriting Scholarship by Image Magazine. She received a Poetry Scholarship from Hudson Valley Writers Center in 2022. Her poetry has been published in journals such as *Post Mortem Press, Lady Blue, LullabyZine, Etchings Press, Hare's Paw* and *The Lanthorn.* You can find her music on all streaming platforms under the moniker "Sorrow Estate".

❖   Laura Jane Round (she/they) is a writer and performance poet from the Black Country in England A Liverpool John Moores University alumni, their work focuses on class, identity and the complicated language of the body. Their second chapbook, 'TEATH', was released by Alien Buddha Press in 2022. Round is bisexual

- ❖ Lawrence Miles is a poet living in White Plains, NY. He has recently been published in Poets Live Fourth Anthology, 2022 New Generation Beats Anthology and Four Feathers Press' Sounds of Southern California: Poetry of Music.

- ❖ Linda lives in Ireland with her husband and her two children. She is a primary school teacher who has a passion for writing. Her work can be found on her Instagram account @sweet.focail

- ❖ Elizabeth Yew (She/They) writes under the nickname "Liz Yew" and has had poems published physically and digitally since she began focusing on writing poetry. Liz grew up in Hong Kong and is now working on a BA in English literature and creative writing in the UK. She never understood poetry growing up, but since discovering Sylvia Plath's work, their own collection of depressing and reflective poetry, along with occasionally cheerful ones, quickly grew. However, being away from home does mean missing her dogs, which they compensate for with her newfound hobby of crocheting.

- ❖ Lucía Retta is a writer and interdisciplinary artist of mixed European, Mexican, and Indigenous heritage. She holds an MFA from Brown University and currently lives and works on the land of the Narragansett people in Providence, Rhode Island, where she teaches creative writing.

- ❖ Marisa Silva-Dunbar's work has been published in *The Bitchin' Kitsch, ArLiJo, Pink Plastic House, Sledgehammer Lit, Analogies & Allegories Literary Magazine.* Her second chapbook, "When Goddesses Wake," was released in December, 2021 *from Maverick Duck Press.* Her first full-length collection, "Allison," was recently published by *Querencia Press.* You can find her on Twitter and Instagram @thesweetmaris. To check out more of her work go to www.marisasilvadunbar.com

- ❖ Meghan King is a Jersey born and raised writer. Her poem Sovereign Hope was featured in *NJ Bards Poetry Review 2022 by Local Gems Press.* She writes poetry and nonfiction on the resilience of the human spirit. Meghan enjoys cooking, reading, and road trips. Wanderlust runs through her veins. Coffee an elixir, laughter medicine, strength in her roots. She holds to the belief in being able to change the tide.

- ❖ M.F. is an Indigenous queer writer, from Poundmaker Cree Nation. Their work focuses on urban Indigeneity, intergenerational trauma, and complex family systems. She is currently an undergraduate student at the University of British Columbia.

- ❖ Michael Gigandet is a lawyer living on a farm in middle Tennessee. He has been published by the *Dead Mule School of Southern Literature, Reedsy, Spelk Fiction, OrangeBlushZine, Transfigured* and *Potato Soup Journal.* He has published stories in collections by *Palm Sized Press, Pure Slush* and *Down In The Dirt.*

- ❖ Mirjam Mahler writes poems and stories. She finds great joy in reading the words from others and in helping others find their words. She was born in Berlin, Germany, raised in Madrid and Barcelona, Spain, attended university in Santa Barbara, California, USA and in Barcelona and is now living in the south of Germany. Mirjam offers workshops to introduce others to the short form poetry she love and hosts four book clubs in two languages. Her poems have been published in three anthologies in 2022 and she is working on publishing her own collection. You can find her @mirjamwrites on Instagram and at mirjamwrites.com

- ❖ nat raum (b. 1996) is a disabled artist, writer, and genderless disaster from Baltimore, MD. They're a current MFA candidate, the editor-in-chief of fifth wheel press, and the author of *you stupid slut* (Dream Boy Book Club) and *specter dust* (Bullshit Lit), among others. Find them online: natraum.com/links.

- ❖ Nazmi is an aspiring writer and a fervent fan of sneaking out of events expeditiously. She's currently pursuing BA in Psychology and when she isn't oscillating between writing and college, she's catering to her propensity of analyzing movies, tv shows and albums.

- ❖ Nicholas Olah has self-published three poetry collections, Where Light Separates from Dark, Which Way is North and Seasons, the third of which also includes his photography. His work has been published in *Humana Obscura* and *Duck Head Journal*, and accepted for *Resurrection Magazine*, which will publish in February 2023. Check out his work on Instagram at @nick.olah.poetry or visit him on Etsy at https://www.etsy.com/shop/nickolahpoetry.

- ❖ Nicole Garner is Adjunct Professor of Philosophy at Ursuline College. Her research and teaching interests are in the areas of French existentialism, queer theory, and ecophilosophy. She is an activist and advocate who focuses on the LGBTQ+ community as well as on wildlife. Nicole is a wildlife photographer who uses photography to highlight the beauty of the creatures around us who are at risk due to destruction of the environment. Her photos have been shown at Wasmer Gallery and area cafes.

- ❖ Paloma Mckim is a graduate and poet based in Paris. Her poetry often focuses on sexuality, relationships, and celebrating the ordinary and often less savoury aspects of the mind and life. She regularly performs poetry at Au Chat Noir's spoken word evening as well as at Culture Rapide bar. Previous publications include the *Feminist Library's Queer Zine, Curious Publishing Woman's Issue, Unfiltered Zine, Potted Purple Magazine, Teller Magazine, Polemical Magazine, Sunday Mornings at the River's* Covid Anthology among others.

- ❖ R.H. Alexander is the pen name of poet Keith Hagen. He lives in Northern Wisconsin and since 2020 has been published in a number of literary journals, anthologies and quarterlies including *The Passengers Journal, Humans of the World Blog, Train River Anthologies, Oprelle Publications* and the *Quillkeepers Press*. His chapbook *Confessions from Eden* was published in February 2022 by

Rare Earth Ink publications. *Alexander was* a 2022 Best of the Net prize nominee. More of his work can be found on Instagram at #R.H.Alexander.

❖ Sara Wiser (she/her/hers) is a current Drama and Transcultural Literature student at The American University in Washington, DC. Originally from Philadelphia, Sara's work features musings on intimacy, love, loss, intergenerational trauma, sexuality, nature, and girlhood. Find more at www.SaraWiser.com or discover her on Instagram @sara.wiser

❖ Sarah Jeannine Booth is a poet and third year BFA writing student. Because of an irresistible obsession with forests, nature seeps into most of Sarah's writing. She lives on the west coast of Canada with her husband and their golden doodle. Connect with her on Instagram @sarahjeanninewrites.

❖ Sophie Morelli is a queer writer residing in Lake Placid, New York. She is the Director of the Lake Placid History Museum and enjoys dismantling the racist and sexist foundations of her small town. She possesses a Bachelor's Degree and a Master's Degree, both from SUNY Potsdam.

❖ Steve Denehan lives in Kildare, Ireland with his wife Eimear and daughter Robin. He is the author of two chapbooks and four poetry collections. Winner of the Anthony Cronin Poetry Award and twice winner of Irish Times' New Irish Writing, his numerous publication credits include *Poetry Ireland Review* and *Westerly*.

❖ Stuti (she/ her) is an Indian writer & musician, who lives in Dubai, UAE. She writes primarily about the human experience and emotions. Being passionate about travel, she loves to weave different cultures and her heritage into her writing. In 2022, she won the International Westmoreland Award for Short Fiction & The International Allingham Festival Prize for Poetry. She also received an honourable mention in the International Globe Soup Short Memoir Contest and was long-listed for the International Erbacce & International Gloucestershire Poetry Contests. She previously has an honourable mention in the 2021 Annual Haiku Competition by The Society of Classical Poets and has been published by them, *Sky Island Journal, Celestite Poetry, Moss Puppy Magazine, Slice of Life Lit Mag, Duck Duck Mongoose Mag,* and *Sonder Magazine*. She has also been published in the Unchaining Freedom Anthology Trilogy by *Ink Gladiators Press* (2022) and First Line Poets Anthology (2022). Stuti is an animal lover and has a fur baby whose name is Yuki.

❖ Supravo Rahman (he/him) is an aspiring writer from Bangladesh, He is currently an undergraduate student at University College London. His writing mostly involves science-fiction and fantasy, of which he is also an avid reader. Besides reading and writing, he also enjoys traveling.

- ❖ Tony-Lydia McKinney (pronouns: they/them/she), also known as The Prodigy Truth, is a 30 year-old trans/non-binary poet, performing artist, activist, and domestic violence survivor. They are ranked #4 in Houston's '22-'23 competitive poetry slam season. T. Lydia attended Texas State University majoring in Communication Studies and minoring in Theatre. They previously worked as a residential instructor for Texas School for the Blind and served as a child abuse investigator in the Texas capital county for 2.5 years, before becoming a full-time independent artist. They are currently finalizing their first full-length collection of poetry, "The Corona Tapes", which details the diary of a nameless, genderless black-indigenous person coping with the trials of dysphoria during the pandemic.

- ❖ Val (she/they) is a college student studying English and education. She is an advocate for many different social issues, including Deaf education, body acceptance, immigration, women's rights, and LGBT+ rights. She currently resides in north Texas with her cat, Polkadot.

- ❖ Wesley R. Bishop is an assistant professor of Public and American history at Jacksonville State University, Alabama. He is the founding and managing editor of the *North Meridian Review: A Journal of Culture and Scholarship*.

- ❖ Zary Fekete has worked as a teacher in Hungary, Moldova, Romania, China, and Cambodia. They currently live and work as a writer in Minnesota. Some places they have been published are *Goats Milk Mag, Journal of Expressive Writing, SIC Journal, Reflex Fiction*, and *Zoetic Press*. They enjoy reading, podcasts, and long, slow films. Twitter: @ZaryFekete

www.ingramcontent.com/pod-product-compliance
Lightning Source LLC
Chambersburg PA
CBHW060913210726
48293CB00006B/2084